G A L A X Y * B O U N D 01

The Year before the End

Sovereign Earth Book 1 of 6

Vidar Hokstad

The Year before the End

Chapter 1	1
Chapter 2	15
Chapter 3	21
Chapter 4	28
Chapter 5	32
Chapter 6	39
Chapter 7	43
Chapter 8	47
Chapter 9	53
Chapter 10	56
Chapter 11	59
Chapter 12	63
Chapter 13	68
Chapter 14	74
Chapter 15	78
Chapter 16	83
Chapter 17	86
Chapter 18	91
Chapter 19	97
Chapter 20	101
Chapter 21	106

Chapter 22 110

Chapter 23 114

Chapter 24 117

Chapter 25 122

Chapter 26 126

Chapter 27 129

Chapter 28 131

Chapter 29 133

Chapter 30 137

Chapter 31 141

Chapter 32 144

Chapter 33 146

Chapter 34 148

Chapter 35 152

Chapter 36 157

Chapter 37 159

Chapter 38 163

Chapter 39 167

Chapter 40 172

Chapter 41 174

Chapter 42 178

Chapter 43 183

Chapter 44   187

Chapter 45   192

Chapter 46   196

Chapter 47   199

Chapter 48   202

Chapter 49   204

Chapter 50   207

Chapter 51   210

Chapter 52   214

Chapter 53   218

Chapter 54   220

Epilogue   223

If you enjoyed this book . . .   225

Chapter 1

The tallest tower of Tharsis City extended beyond the outer dome like a gleaming monument.

Zara Ortega looked out over the city, recalling the first time she had seen Mars, about thirty years ago. She had been just a child, accompanying her father on a business trip.

They had visited several small settlements together, and she had devoured every little scrap of information she could learn about them on the trip from Earth.

Back then, the colonists were still scattered across the surface, huddled in the smaller craters and canyons that could be domed without too much imported material for structural reinforcement.

Most buildings had been dour and reddish-brown, made from a form of locally produced concrete. The walls were thick to provide radiation shielding, with few and small windows. The settlements looked similar to old adobe-style villages on Earth from the outside.

Often, they were set into crater walls, most of the actual rooms carved out of the ground and reinforced.

She remembered how even with the domes, red dust penetrated everywhere. She had still found Mars-dust in the spine of her books weeks after she returned to Earth with her father.

When she had looked out from the room high up in the hotel they had stayed in for a precious few days before they went back home, the landscape she could see in the distance still contained just desert and mountains with the odd, faint glint of another small dome.

It had been the last trip they went on together before her parents divorced. And so she stood there for a few minutes; lost in the memories of that trip.

She could not help but be in awe at how different everything looked now.

In those early days of the Mars Colony, the construction took a *triple-layer* approach in most places. This approach had created a very distinctive and claustrophobic appearance to it all and it had been firmly imprinted in her memories.

From outside, on the ship, the first thing she had seen were the low-pressure, seemingly flimsy outer domes, that her books had told her could contain just enough air pressure with manageable amounts of leakage to hold on to just enough heat. These flimsy domes were sufficient to make it viable to go outside with the breathing mask, a small canister, and a suitable work suit rather than a full spacesuit, and which also created an environment allowing a limited range of vegetation imported from mountain areas on Earth to slowly spread out.

You still didn't want to spend much time out without more gear because the lack of a magnetosphere still meant you would get bathed in more radiation than you should.

Inside the outer domes, you would find one or more smaller inner domes with a more rigid structure and higher air pressure—equivalent to a high altitude city on Earth—that would cover a cluster of buildings and their immediate surroundings. Here, you could drop the oxygen canisters but could easily become out of breath if you were new to Mars.

Finally, the innermost layer consisted of fully sealed building complexes with airlocks.

The latter a safety feature in case both the outer and inner domes were seriously breached. A design that had served the colony well through a number of minor accidents, only a few of which caused a loss of life despite the harsh environment.

Many of these building complexes were connected via underground or above-ground tunnels, allowing one to move between them even in the case of a breach of a dome.

The day the Mars gate came online, it all changed forever. It was the first large demonstration of how dramatically all of the solar system would change—all of humanity—when the Earth-Centauri gate came online.

Transport costs dropped by more than 90% in the first month alone, as a transport ship that could previously manage one return trip every few years, could now do several trips a month, or even several per week for smaller ships with quick turnaround times in-orbit or on Earth.

When Zara visited Mars again a few years after the Earth-Mars gate came online, Mars had already become a giant construction site, and it still was, spreading out from the main transport hubs and covering more and more of the planet's surface, though still a tiny proportion compared to Earth.

Since then, the tiny domes near mining complexes and scientific stations had become a museum of what Mars used to be like.

Advances coming out of the Centauri information transfers allowed for larger, stronger, lighter domes—amongst many other things—and the gates allowed for transferring massive quantities of construction material and equipment. First from Earth, then, as the belt gates came online, from the asteroid belt as well.

By 2121, they had gone one better and started wholesale transfers of large chunks of smaller asteroids. Well placed charges on suitable asteroids would split chunks off, just small enough to put thrusters on one of the asteroid belt gates safely and scoop them up.

Or so the information poster in the arrivals lounge that she'd been reading while waiting for her transfer told her, but Zara had seen these transfers happen first hand on jobs in the belt too.

Large asteroid chunks were flown in; excruciatingly slow at first as attached engines would start nudging them towards the belt gates.

Even before they arrived in Mars or Earth space, automated ore-processors were attached to break the whole thing into pieces, analyze the contents, and sort it to feed to different extractors or smelters suitable for the predominant material in each piece. Then grinding the remains once they were unable to extract more minerals into aggregate that would be used for concrete.

High-value materials would be lowered to the planet below, while bulk materials, like the aggregate or less valuable metals plentiful enough on the surface not to be worth dropping down, would usually be used for in-orbit construction of space stations, jump-gates, or ships.

The use of concrete for in-space structures had been totally unheard of previously. While additives such as micro silica that could extend the lifetime of concrete structures into the thousands of years were known of, building with concrete used to require too much mass.

Suddenly, moving the mass had become far cheaper, and reinforced sulfur concrete with silica and other additives had become attractive building material. In particular, it had become viable as an alternative for shielding and structural support for space stations—for ships they still increased overall mass too much; fuel costs and thrust still put a cost premium on extra mass on ships—as well as for interior walls.

These materials were not new—they were first developed for use on Luna Colony long before the early parts of the colony had even been built back in the 21st century. As a result, large parts of Luna Colony consisted of houses of sulfur concrete made from Lunar regolith, and boosting concrete from the Moon had, in turn, been mooted many times, but the gates made even boosting mass from the Moon's low gravity well seem expensive.

It made far larger stations than before cost effective in places where pure metal structures would have been too expensive. The giant Vanguard II station in Lunar space was one of the first to make use of large-scale concrete construction.

Back on Mars, the result of the sudden inexpensive material combined with the fast and cheap transport of people caused the Mars Colony to swell from tens of thousands to tens of millions in three decades, expanding faster each year. Seemingly all of Mars were employed in construction to pave way for the constant influx.

Zara didn't particularly care about the details of why Mars had changed so much, though she appreciated how, during approach, you could now see streaks of green spreading out in fractal patterns from where domed tunnels were stretching out from the larger city-domes to smaller domes. Further tunnels expanded outwards to small mining sites or new construction sites, allowing life to sprout in larger and larger portions of the long-dead Mars deserts.

She also enjoyed the ever taller towers stretching up toward the sky. Mars' low gravity allowed the advances in materials to go much further.

***

Pavonis Mons, the smallest of the volcanoes on the Tharsis Bulge, stood around 14 km above Mars' mean surface level. A midget amongst the Tharsis volcanoes and their giant cousin at the Western edge of the plateau—Olympus Mons—which was the largest peak in the solar system, gently sloping up to a summit 27 km above mean surface level.

Pavonis Mons' 5 km deep circular caldera, and the gentle outer slopes of the volcano, had made it an ideal location to situate a large domed city. And, with the rapid growth of Mars, it had become the location for the colony capital.

The dome of Pavonis Mons was the largest structure in the solar system; in effect built as a giant inflatable, initially held up by a range of towers near the rim, and gradually allowed to rise when the air pressure inside rose high enough to allow it. Only material science advances from the Centauri data allowed for a material strong enough and light enough to be suitable.

The caldera was larger than most large Earth cities by a substantial factor, with a usable surface area about a hundred times larger than the island of Manhattan. The dome of Pavonis Mons rose up to about 7500 m above the lowest area of the caldera.

Yet, several of the tallest central towers of the city, named Tharsis after the region, were now rising above the surrounding volcano, with the tallest of them all—at 6500 m tall—extending 1500 m up above, gleaming in the sunlight, and leaving only 1000 m to the top of the giant outer dome.

That one gleaming tower penetrated it and rose beyond even the confines of the other dome.

She had heard there was talk of even higher towers, after the feasibility of extending past the dome itself had been proven by the Independence Tower—the name a direct challenge to Earth rule—bracing the dome and buildings against each other.

Currently, Tharsis City had only a few million inhabitants, but the city's growth was accelerating. The last year alone, population rose by nearly a million and domed space was at a premium. With the construction cost of these towers dropping steadily, they had become the preferred way of expanding the city, with the government jealously guarding the surrounding domed real estate for future expansion to delay the inevitable costs of excavation and additional domes.

As a result, Tharsis was a city with a feeling of compactness to it, in the same way as other super-dense areas, with the same apparent contradiction of towers reaching from the sky surrounded by wilderness, like Hong Kong.

Eventually, the Mars Colonial Government hoped to terraform the whole planet to make the true *outside* habitable to some extent or other.

Some of the efforts had started yielding success at getting genetically modified lichen and small plants to start spreading outside too. But terraforming had to be considered a multi-generation project if it were ever to have sufficient effect to allow dome-free construction.

***

Zo—nicknamed after her initials—waited for the shuttle to her hotel while looking out at the city from the large observation windows.

The terminal was set on the western edge of the rim of Pavonis Mons, and the building made the most of the location, with spectacular views of the gentle red slopes down to the Tharsis Plateau to the west, and the view of the caldera and the city to the east.

She was there to discuss a job; the kind of job you discuss only face to face. Not so much out of fear of someone listening in, as she knew even if someone were able to beat the encryption, they would not really care—she would not be discussing any rebellions or other matters that might interest anyone.

Meeting face to face was about trust for her, and about figuring out if her counterpart was telling the truth about the job. Or at least as much of the truth as was necessary for her to feel okay about taking it.

She considered herself quite flexible. Most of the jobs she signed up for were bounty hunts that may or may not have been legal.

Some involved smuggling. Drugs at times. The occasional weapons. As long as it wasn't anything too nasty, she didn't particularly care if laws were broken. Making a living as an independent without being reduced to shuttle traffic in near-Earth space did not allow you to be picky.

She had become *Zo*—few of her crew ever used her full name or title, as they were all family to her—about twenty years previously.

She had signed on to what she expected to be a very ordinary transport job with what turned out to be a crew mainly consisting of mercenaries. They took on jobs that saw them fly in and out of the embers of the many conflicts that were slowly ending as Earth forcefully re-asserted its supremacy on the back of the gate tech.

The crew she flew with fanned the remaining flames—flying in weapons to rebel groups and others without asking questions. Every successful mission prolonged a conflict enough to secure demand for further shipments. She wasn't happy with it, but not unhappy enough to give up the first job to give her a decent income.

They soon became her first real family.

One time, after she'd been at the job for two years and worked her way up to navigation, they made a mistake and didn't vet their client well enough. They were caught in an ambush arranged by other arms dealers looking to steal their shipment.

Their leader and the senior officers of the ship were killed. Zo and two mechanics were the only survivors. They barely got back to the ship, and she became the ship's new captain by default as the most senior person standing.

From then on, that was what she was. They managed to get away, shook off the pursuers, and hid in the belt for a while, making repairs. She managed to get a new crew together at one of the smaller belt stations. Not as hardcore—she'd not become a pacifist, but she wanted to live, not die supplying warring factions in wars she didn't believe in.

Meeting face to face was also about making sure she could recognize the client's representative if she had a reason to track him down once the job was done.

Say, if they didn't make the promised final payment, or someone decided an ambush was a good idea.

Zo liked to tell the story of how she became captain to these clients, and show them the long, uneven scar from a plasma burn along her left arm that was given to her as she was escaping, and also to point out to them how the first job of her new crew—the way they proved their worth to her—had been to hunt down those who had ambushed her previous crew and kill them.

It was her one firm rule: any of her crew died, someone would pay.

Then, she pointed out that they had hunted down the man who had arranged the job that had led them into the ambush.

Zo herself had used a plasma rifle and burned off piece after piece of his body—cauterizing the wounds so he would not bleed out too quickly.

First a hand. Then a foot. His genitals. She had cut the man fifteen times before his body could not take any more and he died.

The captain didn't know exactly what the cause of death was in the end—she was not a doctor, as she pointed out, and hadn't waited to find out what a doctor might say.

When she told this story, her face would contract as if she herself felt the pain she'd inflicted. She did not enjoy it, but it was necessary, she stressed, while staring at the person she told the story to, and she always does what is necessary.

They ejected the man, and the pieces, into space.

Space is big—he would not be found. But he would keep floating around out there.

***

The shuttle trip from the terminal was short and uneventful, and Zo enjoyed the view. After the gleaming towers of Tharsis City had started to rise to substantial height, the new shuttle had been built to cut travel times by gently sloping down to a couple of kilometers over the caldera floor, then straight out into the air, connecting with several of the towers kilometers above the ground, each providing a station, and providing interconnection to other buildings by a series of foot bridges.

The result was to turn the height of the towers, that had fast become a disadvantage, into an advantage: the first truly three-dimensional city in the solar system.

8

It was effectively turning Tharsis City into a single meta-building—a structure where the building blocks were buildings rather than bricks.

But she was going all the way to ground level, and when she arrived at the station and stepped outside, she marveled at just how huge the dome felt, and how it was nothing like what she remembered from childhood.

Back then, even *outside*, the domes were small enough to make it feel as if you were still in a large hangar-style building. A feeling exacerbated by relatively visible support structures and by being set deep into steep craters or valleys.

Now, it felt like being outdoors. Properly outdoors. It helped that the Pavonis Mons caldera sloped very gently, so it was not at all like being at the bottom of some steep valley with mountains all around, but like having distant mountain edges occasionally visible between buildings far away.

There was even some occasional minor cloud formation—the dome was large enough to have some minor weather.

Due to the height of the buildings, most of Tharsis did not have the old design of smaller domes covering the buildings. Instead, streets were increasingly covered between twenty and thirty stories up by transparent ceilings of the same materials used for the domes connecting the buildings, and the air pressure was high enough to make walking outside, even without an oxygen supply, quite pleasant. Those who did wear breathing equipment wore only the lightest of masks, slightly augmenting the air pressure rather than providing it all.

Above the covered height, the buildings themselves incorporated extra seals.

She found the hotel without any problem. The hotel was basic, with a design she noted was a kind of faux Mars adobe style, referencing the small, early colonial buildings heavily while clearly having been built with the newest materials.

She checked in and found her room. After freshening up, she still had a couple of hours before the meeting and decided to spend it strolling around the streets around the hotel and just take in the sights.

***

She walked into the hotel restaurant at the agreed time and looked around.

Hotel restaurants have a way of looking the same wherever you are, whatever planet, moon or space station you might visit. The décor was slightly dated but well maintained. Indistinct colors chosen to be inoffensive, coupled with the same type of pattern used on public transport to minimize the appearance of stains and wear if the place was toward the cheaper end.

The furniture, simple enough to serve a dual or triple purpose as a breakfast room in the morning and conference rooms as needed, without being perfect for any one of the purposes.

Her client was waiting at a table near the entrance. The moment she noticed that there were three large, rough-looking men with poorly concealed weapons that were trying and failing to be inconspicuous a couple of tables over, her steps became more apprehensive and her muscles tensed.

Her client was not likely to be naïve enough not to have spotted them, which meant, that as he was sitting there calmly, he had been the one to bring them.

Bringing muscle to a meeting like this was unusual. Most of her clients did not feel the need to bring any.

If it happened, it was rarely a good sign. Certainly not when they were trying to hide in play view in the background. And certainly not when they got up and started marching aggressively toward her as these guys just did.

She wondered if she'd been set up by law enforcement. As far as she knew she wasn't wanted on Mars. Some of the more shady stations were run by the types who didn't care much for jurisdiction and would happily line the pockets of the right people to get them to help out. Mars was full of "helpful" law enforcement. She thought the men looked a bit on the rough side for Mars law enforcement, though.

Of course, some of the *law enforcement* on the shadier stations were as close to well-trained, proper law enforcement, as the average park attendant, and would also not care about jurisdiction even if the station operator had managed to get them approved as *community support officers*.

Effectively, they were privatized police without all the same powers, but infinitely cheaper for Earth and with entirely the same ego as real police officers, often coupled with an inferiority complex that tended to make them a lot more dangerous.

Before Zo had a chance to turn and run, she could feel a gun against her back. Apparently, there were four large, rough-looking men with poorly concealed weapons and she'd done a poor job paying attention on the way in. *Shit.*

"Thank you for coming, Captain Ortega. Don't do anything stupid, and you will walk away from this. We don't want to hurt you."

Her client walked up to her with an outstretched hand; one the captain ignored.

"What the hell is this about? My instructions were clear."

The man kept his hand outstretched a while longer.

"It's about a job. Just as you were told. All you've been told is true. The . . . extra staff is here because, well, we have trust issues and we want to impress upon you exactly what the consequences might be if our limited trust is misplaced."

The man shrugged his shoulders.

"Consider this a show of force to demonstrate we are very serious people."

They walked over to the table her client had sat at and the captain sat down in between two of the much bigger men. By the size of them, she judged them to be local Mars-born muscle, well above average height for Earth.

Likely hired for the occasion, rather than brought in by the client, who as far as she knew, had come from Earth to meet in *neutral territory*.

The man was apparently not going to introduce himself, and Zo knew better than to ask for a name that was not volunteered.

"Have you heard about Sovereign Earth?"

Zo nodded. Sovereign Earth was a political movement arguing that Earth should not, under any circumstance, allow independence for colonies elsewhere in the solar system, argued for not completing the Earth-Centauri gate, and for extensive militarization.

She shared some of their fears of what the gate would bring. Sometimes she even wondered if the Centauri wanted to use the gate to invade. She was more skeptical of their views on Earth supremacy in the system, but she'd also seen first-hand the violence of a number of independence movements over the years.

"One of our supporters found evidence of communication between Mars and Centauri that proves pro-independence forces on Mars will act as a fifth column if the Centauri invades once the gate opens, as long as the Centauri grants Mars independence. That is part of the reason we're here; to investigate. It's also part of the reason for my . . . friends here."

Zo didn't know what to think. She thought the independence movements were ill thought through, but she wasn't aware of any groups that seemed like they'd be prepared to go as far as selling out Earth like that.

"Surely, if you have evidence of that, it should be broadcast everywhere?"

"It should. I'm glad we agree. But there's a problem."

The man leaned closer, as if what he was about to tell her was more secret, which didn't seem very likely given what he'd already said.

"As you know, forging video evidence is trivial these days, and so it's hard to get people to believe it. Especially if it is coming from a political group."

He threw his hands up. It was true faked *evidence* of all kinds for various supposed scandals popped up all the time, only to be revealed as having been manufactured with software, and it had desensitized people to it.

"So, our mole obtained a physical copy of some of their plans, complete with fingerprints, and sealed it in a courier capsule."

Zo leaned forward this time, suddenly more interested. If they actually had evidence of something like this, it would change the politics of the entire solar system.

"Unfortunately, he had an accident."

The man scratched his chin. "If it was an accident."

He stared intently at Zo now.

"He died on Vanguard Station two days ago, and when we had someone poke around, it turns out the capsule was put in the vault in C&C alongside the rest of his belongings pending an inquest. We're worried it wasn't an accident and that someone will . . . appropriate the capsule."

"What do want me to do about it?"

"We looked into getting the inquest expedited and his belongings released, but they were not very . . . helpful about it."

The way he said it made Zo think what he meant was that the coroner on Vanguard wasn't easy enough to bribe.

"We need you to go in and get it."

"You want us to break into Vanguard?"

"I wouldn't put it quite like that, but yes."

"You're serious? You realize it's one of the most fortified stations in the system? And Vanguard II, *the* most fortified station in the system is right nearby?"

"Well, quite. That's why we offered the amount we mentioned."

They had offered a very substantial amount. Several times what Zo was used to being paid.

"We also obviously don't want you to outright attack the station."

Zo looked at him with an exasperated expression. "It's not just how to get *in*. Getting into the station is easy. Anyone can get in. The problem is the combination of getting to C&C where the vault is, *and* getting in the weapons and equipment to make that part possible."

"I realize that. We came to you because our normal associates think it can't be done."

"I'm not sure if *I* am convinced it can be done. You realize the C&C on Vanguard is in the central spire, right?"

"That was one of the problems mentioned by our associates, yes."

He looked annoyed, having clearly been through these objections before. Probably more than once.

"Then you understand breaking in means getting past chokehold after chokehold. That place was built to be impossible to take, and you want us to break into the most difficult place to get to in the whole station."

Once the client told her what the job involved, she had immediately considered saying no, but she was a bit intrigued too. Both because of the reason for the job, and the sheer challenge of it. As she was going through

13

the difficulties, she realized she was talking herself into wanting to see if they could pull it off.

"And if we get captured?"

"You'll be on your own, of course. We can't be associated with that."

Zo nodded. That wasn't unusual for the type of jobs she took. But the stakes here were higher.

She grilled him for another half an hour, which he spent patiently answering questions.

About Sovereign Earth, about the Mars independence groups, and about the Centauri threat. And what he told her scared her as well.

She told her story, to stress how she would not tolerate any bullshit. He sat patiently through that too, nodding along, without any noticeable signs of fear.

Zo didn't have any ethical issues about breaking into Vanguard Station's vault and stealing the capsule they asked her to steal, but it was stupidly risky compared to the type of jobs they normally carried out.

An ex-military station with much of the gear still in place, owned by an extremely wealthy conglomerate which highly valued its reputation, manned by top-range security teams and within striking distance of the largest collection of military ships in the solar system was not the type of place one would usually break into if they valued a long and healthy life.

But if they were right, it was a chance to do something meaningful. Something that would save lives.

"You have until this evening to decide—as you can tell, this is time sensitive, so if you don't want the job, we need to find someone else quickly. Good day. We will be in touch."

The client—or rather his representative—rose and strode out, while his muscle filed out after him.

Chapter 2

We first learned that we were not alone on March 13th, 2105.

That was the date that the old, half-forgotten SETI project received the first transmission from near Alpha Centauri.

That it was from Alpha Centauri was perhaps one of the biggest surprises at first. Since it was so close—just a bit over four light years away, we had listened for broadcasts from there for so long without any result, that we were just continuing to listen out of a neighborly politeness of sorts.

Nobody really expected that it would be from Alpha Centauri we'd suddenly pick up broadcasts after this many years of silence. The odds against a civilization not having been broadcasting and then suddenly starting to broadcast this close to when we started listening seemed huge.

But there it was. And it was not something possible to doubt. One day it was not there, and the next it was, as if we'd been out in a quiet forest at night listening for a whisper only to have someone put a megaphone to our ear and start yelling. Whoever it was wanted to be heard—it was an extremely high-powered signal, given the distance.

The broadcast went on for six months before it started repeating itself. It started with simple mathematical patterns. Counts in a variety of number bases. Fundamental sequences such as Fibonacci numbers. Then it switched to physics—the number of electrons, neutrons, protons of the elements. Representations of a number of universal constants.

The first week of broadcasts was clearly intended primarily to make it very obvious to any listener that what they had picked up was not noise, nor *leakage* from broadcasts not intended for outside listeners.

This was a beacon.

The scientists involved were ecstatic for two reasons: Finally contact. And their ideas about how to introduce ourselves to aliens had been validated by an alien species sending us all of the things we ourselves had been broadcasting as a demonstrator of intelligence.

After the first hour, SETI had put out the first press release. Within a day, every news organization in the world was carrying it, and professional and amateur astronomers the world over were tuning in.

But why had it just suddenly started?

The broadcast contained a number of regularly repeated elements. The first week of data repeated every ten weeks or so—presumably to make sure that someone catching the tail-end of a sequence would not dismiss the more densely encoded middle sections as noise.

The content in between repeated too, but on a much longer cycle, and more and more rarely the further in we got.

Even with the extensive and carefully structured set of *dictionaries* of various kinds, and despite the fact that the data was clearly structured to try to make it as easy as possible to decode, it took about a year into the broadcasts before enough was decoded to be able to do proper, full translations, sufficient to tell us who these aliens were, and why they had only now started broadcasting.

In the meantime, scientists the world over had already learned a lot of new things from the fragments we had been able to decode in the meantime.

The *Centauri*, as the news-media had dubbed them the moment the discovery was made public, were in fact not from Alpha Centauri at all, but from a system closer to the Galactic Core. The transmissions did not give a precise location for their home world.

The unexpected and sudden start of transmissions was not because these *Centauri* had suddenly discovered radio and started their own SETI equivalent, but because they were merchants seeking new trading partners.

According to the transmissions, the beacon was part of a faster-than-light jump-gate that had just been brought online near Alpha Centauri as part of a many-centuries-long project of expanding their gate network in what the transmissions described as, loosely translated, *the sparsely populated outer rim of the galaxy* in the hope of enabling trade and technological exchange with civilizations not yet tied in to the larger galactic trading routes.

This introduction of sorts provided a rather depressing solution to the Fermi paradox (if there are aliens all over the place, why are they not here yet?):

The galaxy was indeed teeming with life, but the reason they'd not come here yet was that nobody had a particularly compelling reason to. It turned out we live in a sparsely populated galactic backwater, outside of trading routes established for millennia.

The expansion outside of the gate network was apparently slow and expensive—requiring sending an expensive high-mass ship containing core material for one end of a gate pair at sub-light speeds to each new location.

Ancient civilizations once spread like wildfire, but when they met, the exploration rate dropped rapidly. Trade beat exploration any day. Each new civilization discovered, gave the older ones new systems to explore and trade with, without the inconvenience of roughing it with sub-light ships, giving them progressively less reason to bother going off the gate network.

Who could blame them? The same had happened on Earth, after all. Early civilizations expanded until they met and suddenly had borders to protect or expand, or trade to conduct with each other, and it took millennia before we even had complete-enough maps to know where all the gaps were, much less fill them in. Because, as rewarding as exploration could be, it was also high risk, and so it was undertaken mostly when obstacles stood in the way of trade.

The arrival of the Centauri gate was the interstellar equivalent of a remote, pretty much forgotten, under-developed village finally being told they now had a bus connection to civilization a hundred years after everyone else—if they would just walk for three days to the neighboring village.

The Centauri were making a bet that by *plugging holes* in the gate network, they would discover the odd civilization here and there, that despite not yet having developed gate travel of their own, would be worth trading with, and allow them to increase their influence and wealth.

Alpha Centauri, the documents explained, was one of many such systems picked because they were deemed to be most likely to maximize the chances of a sufficiently advanced civilization being close enough to be capable of getting there in a reasonable time-frame based on preliminary radio surveys.

We did not, and do not, know from where they did these surveys and, at the time, we had no way of knowing whether they were done close enough for any of our transmissions to have reached them at the time the Centauri gate was dispatched. Perhaps, had they heard them, they would have sent one directly to Sol, or perhaps that idea was just our vanity.

What followed, after a lengthy introduction, was their equivalent of an encyclopedia, and then the thing that would truly change everything.

We would not be limited to radio contact with a regular delay of more than four years. We would not be limited to travel to them at sub-light speeds in order to meet them or trade with them.

While the Centauri gate was the nearest, the beacon was there because the Centauri gate was not meant to be the outer reaches of their gate system, but an open interchange point. Neutral ground, subject to *reasonable tolls*.

Data followed, explaining how anyone receiving the signals were welcome to send a gate endpoint to Alpha Centauri, and obtain access via the Centauri gate to the wider gate system.

"Oh, and in case you're backwards savages, what follows includes complete plans for how to build a jump-gate and how to build a suitable transport to send an endpoint. And here're our details so you can tell us when you'll be arriving."

They were a bit more polite about it than that. They didn't actually call us savages, as far as we could tell from our translations, but some experts did suggest the messages were written in a somewhat condescending tone, or possibly the kind of language they would use with children.

Chaos ensued, followed by committees, studies, and complex negotiations conducted at what amounted to an astounding speed given the number of government organizations, politicians, and private companies involved, which led to construction efforts starting only two years later.

By 2113, the first gate core pair had been constructed, and one end had been dispatched. The ship built to the provided specifications would put the gate core on schedule to arrive near Alpha Centauri in 2145.

Meanwhile, one of the largest series of construction projects in human history was starting to churn out smaller gates to connect the scattered Sol-local colonies of humanity and cut travel times with the fastest previously available ships orbit to orbit from days (the Moon), months (Mars) or years (Io, some of the asteroids) to hours—most of which was spent getting to and from the gates.

The colonies boomed. Earth boomed as resources flooded in from the asteroid belt, as transport capacity went through the roof once the expensive transport ships could do a trip in a fraction of the time, and flooded back out to build more colonies as well as in-orbit transit stations and fleets of ships.

But, while the economy boomed, society went through massive upheavals, and politics became a mess. As of 2106, it was clear that we had maybe forty years left until we would no longer be alone. In a sense, we already were not—we soon started actively transmitting towards Alpha Centauri, and in 2115 we received the first answer—the first alien communication addressed directly to us rather than to any random listening civilization.

One of the first parts of the new targeted data stream was a confirmation that a gate would be ready for integration of the gate core that was en route, and a welcome message.

Mass suicides increased as religious cults saw it as the end days, or saw it as salvation and expected passing aliens to pick up their souls, in a repeat of the ancient Heaven's Gate cult that committed suicide in California before the turn of the 21st century.

Politicians argued endlessly about whether we should aggressively build up our military, or trust that the visitors would be peaceful, and about whether we would even have any hope of stopping an invasion if it turned out we faced an aggressor.

Isolationist and militaristic political parties like Sovereign Earth grew from nothing to significant influences.

Alien invasion movies, games, and VR-stories saw a massive resurgence.

In the end, our own local *tests* of gate travel satisfied most of the militarists: while the gate designs were without access controls or other means of restricting travel and we didn't know how to add them, we could blow up our gate, they determined, and cut off any small initial force.

The gates also put an upper limit on the spherical volume of ships, limiting what could be transferred.

If it did result in us blowing the gate up, on one hand we'd be isolated again. On the other hand, it would leave an invading force having to take the

19

long way—sub-light travel—giving us many years of warning even if they had already massed a fleet near Alpha Centauri, based on optimistic assumptions about how rapidly they could accelerate.

Nevertheless, an influential article caused 2145 to become nicknamed as *The End*.

Though, depending on who you asked, they would take the label as anything from a joke to a deadly serious proclamation of impending doom.

It would be the end of isolation and being alone in the universe amongst those who longed for humanity to take its place in the stars.

The end of the world amongst those who expected alien invaders to pour through the gate and kill us all (or possibly just lob an impossibly powerful warhead through).

The end of poverty/war/greed amongst those who expected the gate to open up endless possibilities for new wealth and make humanity find together in its new-found prosperity.

Chapter 3

Before she started planning the operation, she had never once wondered where a space station stores its sewage.

Zo had spent a substantial proportion of her life in space—first as crew on transport ships in the early days of expansion after the gates started coming online and tied Sol closer together than ever before. Then, after the event that propelled her into the captain's seat, piloting her own ship and doing a bit of this and that, including smuggling, transporting passengers, occasional detective work, security detail, and the odd job for law enforcement.

In that time, she had visited most of the space stations that were spreading throughout the solar system (all of the older ones, but these days new ones popped up all the time). But she had never thought about this particular issue. Probably hadn't wanted to.

Few people have thought about where all the nitty gritty, less savory but very necessary services of a major space station are located, or about the layout of a space station at all.

In movies, all the vital stuff is usually sitting right there on the outer hull, as easy targets to be taken out when the movie-enemy attacks. The same hull is also often full of nice, huge observation windows that can crack or be blown apart, and which open onto large open interior spaces that can conveniently cause people to get sucked out into the void.

And, of course, Command and Control. Somewhere nice and visible and exposed, because who doesn't like to ensure the nerve center of the station is easily exposed to weapons fire?

"Shit. Literally and figuratively."

It was quite obvious, really, once she saw the plans, why the station was built the way it was.

There are many concerns when building a station that aren't a worry when building on a planet. For starters, recycling everything. Even in the harsher planetside colonies there is usually some flexibility in this. In particular, there is land to do this away from the habitats.

But, on a space station, options are limited. Moving mass was still expensive even after the massive cost reductions the gate network brought. Space travel still required a lot of fuel, and a lot of products needed to be boosted out of a gravity well too.

A space station can't go dumping all their waste into space because, even ignoring the hazards it would cause to create a fine cloud of assorted waste around a shipping line, the cost of replacing the lost matter is too high.

Even if it is shit.

Then there's the issue of heat. Whenever a side of the station is facing the sun, it needs to account for heating; for stations in the far outer reaches of the system this might be great news, but further in means it is constantly being baked. Whenever it is in shadow, it is *cold*, but not cold like on a planet, because there's not much there to conduct heat away. Talking about it being *cold* in space misses that point. So they're still finding it hard to get rid of excess heat as radiating it away is a slow process.

And any station sufficiently large will get constantly hit by space junk, and constantly face the risk of being hit by ships that fail to dock properly.

"That's it. We'll fail to dock," she said to herself.

Then there's gravity. You want it. And the easiest way of simulating gravity on any semi-stationary object larger than a tin can and smaller than a planet is to spin it.

Fast.

Which makes the outer hull, the floor, and the most practical design: a cylinder. A spinning cylinder has the added advantage of making it harder for unwanted visitors to try to dock where they shouldn't.

"What was that, Captain?" Clarice asked, looking over at the captain.

Zo was back on her ship, on the bridge, and they were currently coasting after a short burn. The crew had been briefed. It was late and most of the crew had gone to bed. They'd come up with a reasonable plan for what to do once inside Vanguard, but they'd not cracked how to get the weapons and tools they needed into the station in the first place.

Clarice was the only one there with her.

***

Clarice Morgan was a young electrical engineer and software developer who served as the navigations officer. She claimed she'd left school to see the colonies, but didn't seem the type. The captain picked her up on Mars after a mission a year or so ago after Clarice spent most of her money and wasn't particularly interested in seeking help from the local government to arrange her return home.

Zo offered to take her back to Earth for free, probably because she was young, petite, and quite pretty in an *I'm going to hurt you if you touch me without permission* kind of way, and the captain had a weakness for young pretty women and liked her attitude.

They always got on well, but nobody on the crew knew for sure if anything had happened between them, and they weren't about to ask as long as neither the captain nor Morgan brought it up.

Either way, Morgan had almost immediately decided she'd rather stay on board than go back to Earth, even if the salary wasn't great and the ship didn't provide anything like what you'd expect if your only previous experience was passenger liners.

***

Spinning the cylinder of a space station or ship to create a perceived gravity leaves the ends of the cylinder as the only viable place to put the docking ports, as lining up with the sides becomes more and more complex the faster the spin, and isn't worth it.

So, that's where you focus the majority of your weapons platforms, and where your guards are stationed.

And a few small, carefully isolated, and airlocked, low-g viewing platforms. Few and small because most people, before they've thought things through, imagine big viewing galleries where they might leisurely take in the majesty of space.

But a station rotating a bit less than once a minute tends to make most people nauseous, especially as the space dead-center was too valuable for docking ports, so you'd face micro-gravity and the appearance of being flung around as well.

"We'll crash into the station on purpose."

The captain grinned at Clarice. Zo didn't grin very often, but it was late, she was tired, and this problem had been driving her crazy.

"What are you talking about?"

The most critical infrastructure, such as Command and Control, life support systems, et cetera are generally positioned near the center axis, and deep enough in from one of the docking ports to be well protected in the case of an attack or accident.

"They won't shoot at us for trying to land on the outer cylinder if we're having an *accident* while trying to dock."

The logical structure of the rest of a space station then, is to place the least valued mass along the outer hull of the cylinder, bottom seen from the inhabitants view on the inside, and use it as a buffer, ideally in a format that lets the station take advantage of the energy converted by the solar film covering the exterior as best as possible, because it's going to spend a lot of effort getting rid of whatever heat makes it through the outer buffer.

Sewage treatment, as it happens, is great for that. If there's damage, nobody cares much except for the maintenance people who will be swearing at station management when ordered to fix it. It makes a decent outer radiation shield and a decent heat-shield through the sheer amount of mass. It can utilize the heat for gas extraction, to help separate the dry matter out for burning or use as fertilizer, and divert the liquid for chemical treatment and further filtering before it gets pumped back into the drinking water supply.

The outer hull contained many other things too, like large hydroponic farms that likewise benefited from using the heat, but it was the sewage treatment plant that had caught the captain's eye, because it was the thing she'd never really thought about.

"We still need to figure out how to breach the hull without triggering any sensors, but that's how we'll attach to the hull in the first place."

"You're fucking insane, Captain. The tangential velocity at the rim of Vanguard is something like 300 km/h . . . But I love it. I'll make the calculations."

"It can wait until the morning, Clarice. Get some rest."

"You know I won't be able to rest now until I've at least done some initial math."

Clarice smiled gently as her irises started glowing faintly blue and illuminated her pale face and straight black hair in a way that made her look ethereal.

Zo rolled her eyes in an exaggerated manner and smiled back.

Most of the crew were augmented in some way, but most in less obvious ways. Visible augmentation was not fashionable in most circles—only techies or those wanting to rebel would wear noticeable augmentation and ignore consideration of the status implications.

Zo knew Clarice had replaced her first eye at eighteen, her second less than a year later. Even most of those who went as far as that opted for eyes that would mimic biological eyes as closely as possible. Clarice's did too, most of the time—but she could change eye color at will, or go for even more dramatic changes. That wasn't why she'd augmented, though.

The rest of the crew settled for wearing contacts that doubled as screens, alternating between overlays or "blacking out" the iris as a polite signal to their surroundings that their whole field of view had been switched to screen mode.

But Clarice's glowed faintly blue and pulsed slowly between different hues as she got busy reprogramming the navigation computer.

Unlike the contact screens, her eyes still took in everything, and computers processed the signal, ready to notify her or switch to regular sight at a moment's notice if something happened. And when she did see, the lenses in her bionic eyes gave her far superior sight—able to widen her viewing angles, zoom in far beyond the capability of biological eyes, as well as improved night vision and various filtering.

When they first met, the captain asked her why. It wasn't like she'd normally need any of that. Maybe now, on her crew, but not back then.

25

Clarice's answer was, "Why not?" To her, technology was its own reason, and her limits on augmentation were down to cost and how exciting they seemed, not whether or not she needed it. The rest of the crew occasionally speculated about what else she had augmented that she hadn't told them about, but didn't dare ask.

Clarice's changes to the navigation computer progressed slowly as Zo brought up a view of the work she was doing to model how they could disable an engine just right to make it seem like an accident, and get it to change their course just enough to have them scrape along the outer edge for a bit without arousing suspicion.

The captain turned off the display and was quietly looking at Clarice, knowing she couldn't see Zo's worried expression (though, Zo reminded herself, she certainly could scan through her eye recordings afterwards).

She was thinking about what they'd gotten themselves in for. Vanguard was not the kind of target she would normally have risked. Their jobs were not always legal, but they were never particularly high risk.

Even when they went in hot, they went after targets where they knew they had the upper hand. The money wasn't as good that way, but so far it had kept them all alive, which was more than many of the other crews in the same line of business could say. Not that they could speak anymore.

Like her own former captain.

The plan was not looking too great already before she had the idea that the only viable way involved intentionally crashing the ship and breaking into the lower levels.

However, she had little choice but to find a way to carry out the job—their past few jobs had been unprofitable, the ship needed repairs, and she needed to make payments.

Her *client* for this job also worried her a bit. While she'd been convinced of the cause, and understood the importance of it, she didn't have a particularly good feeling about the representative they had sent. His body language had been too intense and wired.

She brushed it off. It was too late in any case. She had accepted, and she never backed out.

The captain climbed out of her harness and floated to the hatch leading toward her quarters, leaving Clarice alone to work.

Chapter 4

People still held out hope for artificial gravity, but it was one of many disappointments in the Centauri data: it indicated nobody had found a practical anti-grav mechanism.

Their ship, the *Black Rain*, like most ships other than the expensive passenger liners, didn't attempt to simulate gravity *properly*. Or at all.

It was impractical, especially for small ships, to try to maintain a balance between rotation and counteracting acceleration and deceleration. It was simply not possible to do in any reasonable way without severely limiting your flight patterns in the first place.

Zero gravity allowed for better use of space.

Instead, the bridge was of an unusual design. A sphere mounted in a gyroscope near the center of the ship, where it was best protected. In normal operation it was locked in place, allowing entry and exit through multiple doorways leading to narrow halls connecting it to the crew quarters, storage facilities, engineering, and other necessary functions. When rapid course corrections were required, or during ship turnaround, it could be fully or partially unlocked, orienting itself to ensure *down* was the direction the engines fired. This would, at least, leave people with a reasonably predictable application of the sense of direction of *gravity* when acceleration occurred.

This was an unusual arrangement for a transport ship, which is what the *Black Rain* looked like from the outside. Freighters rarely needed lots of sudden course corrections to, say, avoid weapons fire.

People unfamiliar with space travel have this odd, to spacers anyway, idea that the direction the ship points is *forward* and that *down* is on a right angle to forward.

The captain remembered finding her dad's old science fiction stories as a child, and laughing at how, when her dad was a child, they had imagined space ships as ships, with bridges where people would stand up tall and steady, looking out of large windows—very occasionally having the sense to make them *viewscreens*—to the *front*, with artificial gravity maintaining a *down* that was firmly at a 90-degree angle to the direction of the thrust.

To Zo, it seemed like such a hopelessly optimistic view of space travel from someone who had experienced the cramped, smelly, windowless gyro-mounted bridges on a transport, or—if you were lucky—the much larger rotating sections of a luxury liner. Even they had to deal with the complexities of gravity now and again.

Because, of course, it doesn't work like they thought it would back then. Instead, it worked like it always had, all the way back to the time humans first blasted off in rockets. Depending on engine configuration, the nose of a spaceship can be pointed in any direction, even if the ship continues on its original heading. Which direction feels like *down* is determined by acceleration, not speed.

On slow haulage routes, there might be no *down* at all other than a short initial thrust to accelerate, a short final deceleration when approaching the target, and a few minor burns to orient the ship to a gate or docking port. During those, the crew would be strapped in—in the bridge-sphere or elsewhere. For the rest, they'd have zero-g conditions.

On courier runs, like what the *Black Rain* would normally do, where speed mattered, or on shorter passenger runs, the ship would typically accelerate at whatever rate was economical and fast enough to the halfway point, and then brake the entire rest of the way, providing the experience of gravity other than when turning. Sometimes, if they pushed the engines hard for an extra-large payout, it'd be uncomfortably high-g.

But now, she was coasting, slowly edging closer to Vanguard. Since she was not accelerating, there was no *up* other than the notional *up* created by the orientation of the locked bridge gyro.

Most of the crew preferred low-g or zero-g runs—the entire ship felt smaller in high-g runs, because you were confined to the side that felt like the floor. You also had the hassle of stowing everything to be able to handle turnaround, when the ship would turn mid-journey and start the deceleration burn, with its nose turned back toward the point of departure, and suddenly your ceiling was the floor and vice versa.

Maneuvering around the ship outside of the bridge also became a pain, with lots of climbing up and down between floors. And getting on and off the bridge was only possible when it was locked in place in the right alignment.

29

Bigger luxury ships sometimes placed the whole habitable part of the ship in a gyro to avoid this. In the case of passenger liners, they were often combined with engines to create spin to compensate and to try to create a sensation of gravity that remained reasonably consistent throughout the journey. But straight spin around a single axis is insufficient to prevent perceived gravity from changing during acceleration and deceleration, or when the ship needed to change course.

In any case, nobody could justify those kinds of expensive, high maintenance mechanisms for a cargo ship, which was what the *Black Rain* was. Officially, at least.

***

Grant swore.

Attaching the extra hull plating had taken forever, and he had just lost a sheet of metal and watched it float away.

They were attaching extra plating to make sure there'd be debris when they'd crash into Vanguard, to make it look better. It was meant to be *sloppy* work in that it was meant to come loose. But not while they were attaching it.

He wished he'd not volunteered to do the outside work with Vincent.

The others, at least, did not have to be suited up for hours on end.

Grant went back to the airlock and waited for it to complete its cycle.

"Fuck, I'm sweaty."

"Thanks for the heads up, now you won't get your cuddles." Zo winked at him.

"As if *you*'d get to cuddle me, Cap." Grant winked back.

"Are you getting close?"

"Yeah, just lost a plate. A couple more and we'll be good to go. How about the inside?"

"We're almost done. You know, it does get hot and sweaty in here too . . . Welding in a confined space isn't fun without a suit either."

Grant held up his hands and mouthed an *okay* before putting his helmet back on and grabbing some more plating.

He hated the preparation for missions, and he hated this one even more than usual, but he was quite looking forward to getting to Vanguard. It'd been a long time since they'd taken a job that included any real action and Grant was confident this would get heated.

"Got the last plates," he told Vincent over the comms. Totally pointless pronouncement, as it'd be hard to miss the two big sheets of metal he was maneuvering out of the airlock.

Chapter 5

The captain didn't make a habit of jumping out of her ship. In fact, today would be a first.

After a day of preparations, they had everything ready. A few hours after that, they had adjusted their approach to Vanguard Station to come in at a more plausible speed to avoid arousing suspicion.

Zo was on the bridge, keeping an eye on the monitors. She could do so from most other places on the ship using her contacts, but she liked the tactile feedback of the physical controls and liked seeing her crew react to her commands, so they all still mostly worked from the bridge.

Not least because it made things easier during changes in acceleration if they were all strapped in.

But she wouldn't stay on the bridge this time. As soon as she'd confirmed everything was ready, she left and headed for the cargo bay.

***

Vanguard Station was a former military station that had been bought by some nondescript property conglomerate named Xanadu Chengdu-Sydney Investment Corporation about twenty years ago. It had been refitted as a trading outpost. The military had outgrown it.

Increasing hysteria over the coming gate opening had provided the military with vast extra appropriations, and as a result, the much larger Vanguard II had been constructed over a period of a decade, within visible range from the station as a giant cylinder—constructed as part of the preparations for the opening of the Earth-Centauri gate, to house a full complement of the new Beastmaster class warships.

The Beastmaster ships had been built specifically to match the maximum volume the gate could accommodate, outfitted with some of the biggest, most devastating weapons-platforms built by humanity.

Like throwing rocks at aircraft carriers was one of the phrases opponents had thrown around about the notion that our weapons might make a difference to an alien civilization as advanced as the *Centauri*, and in anger at the vast amount of resources invested in it; but they had been built anyway.

Of course, Vanguard II's extensive military presence also came in handy over the last two decades for the various *peace-keeping* missions that followed the rush of gate construction, allowing Earth to project power and get a firmer grip on the colonies than it had been able to since the first corporate colonization efforts had started breaking government monopolies on colonies in the 2060s.

Officially, all the colonies willingly signed up to form part of the new reformed solar-system-wide super-planetary government—United Sol. Unofficially, flurries of sternly worded, but easily ignored, protests had been lodged about the presence of Earth warships, whose supply lines were considerably eased by having the Vanguard II as an outpost to operate from, while the votes of the various governing bodies of the colonies had been carried out.

***

A few hours after adjusting speed, *Black Rain* entered Vanguard Station controlled space and sent the necessary identification files. Their permission to approach was granted immediately and automatically by the Vanguard security AI.

"Weapons lock. They're not playing, are they?"

The station might be ex-military, but the conglomerate that bought it paid handsomely for security, and had been able to get a license to keep some of the military weapon stations in part due to its location. They liked to make it clear to visiting ships from the outset that trouble is not welcome on Vanguard.

The initial location of the jump-gate, it had been decided, would be in orbit around the moon rather than Earth. In the case the Centauri transmissions all turned to be a ploy to make an invasion possible, it would give slightly more time to respond.

More paranoid forces had suggested putting it much further away—like Jupiter—but this had been deemed impractical and unnecessary, though a gate pair allowing rapid transport to Jupiter-adjacent space was in place.

Vanguard Station had been constructed in-orbit near enough that its weapons platforms would be able to fire at the gate and destroy it with a single salvo.

When the decision had been made to build the five times larger Vanguard II, the original station had been moved further away—far enough from both the gate and Vanguard II that the weapons left would not allow it to fire on either. But, the cynics pointed out, Vanguard II had some hefty mass drivers that could trivially reduce its older cousin to scattered pieces of twisted metal if, say, the station was to fall in the wrong hands.

***

Black Rain approached main engines first, still on a normal-looking deceleration burn. Vanguard approach procedures demanded they come to a stop relative to the station a few klicks out and then have navigational thrusters rotate the ship, and the main thrusters turning back on to give the nudge needed to send it toward the docking port at a speed the much smaller forward retro-thrusters and navigational thrusters could counteract.

It was a somewhat unusual docking procedure. Many of the smaller stations tended to prefer that people decelerated straight up to the docking port.

But this was part of Vanguard's paranoia: when arriving, you had to face them head-on and, even though your weapons were pointed straight at them, their guns were bigger, and had a target lock on you—if you did the same, you'd be blown up. But, if you tried to leave in a hurry, you were forced to back out of their docking port, boosted only by smaller, forward-facing thrusters.

More than one ship had found out that this was intentional, to give them more time to scramble fighters and prepare their weapons platform to target fleeing criminals and have the rail guns tear them apart, before the fleeing ships were even able to flip around and engage their main engines.

"Steady. Just a few more moments."

Suddenly, one of the engines flickered off, and the ship started veering off course. The navigational thrusters and retro-thrusters flickered but failed to fire to counteract the course change.

"*Black Rain*, this is Vanguard Control, what the hell are you doing? You're due to flip."

"Vanguard Control, this is *Black Rain*, stand by . . ."

"Clarice, they're preparing to fire the rail guns . . ."

Morgan shut down the remaining two main thrusters to prevent the ship from accelerating further and going into a spin.

"Vanguard Control, this is *Black Rain*, please do not fire, we are not in control. We don't know what happened. Something happened to our engine control . . . One of our main engines and our navigational engines are not firing. We're coming in hot. Trying to correct."

She tried sounding as if she were panicking and breathless. They waited for Vanguard's reaction.

"They bought it . . . Their main weapons are standing down. They're still painting us with targeting lasers though."

Tension on the bridge eased a bit, but they knew the hard part was just starting.

A moment later, the weak side and front thrusters lit back up and the ship seemed to try to compensate, but the earlier acceleration was too much for the small navigational thrusters to counteract fully.

Morgan upped the desperation in her voice as much as possible while relaying additional details to Vanguard Control, and at the same time carefully tweaking the parameters to account for the odd variable her quick and dirty model didn't anticipate.

She wasn't at all desperate. She had an uncanny ability to stay calm no matter what. The only hint of stress those who knew her well might pick up was a slight pursing of her lips. In this case, hurtling toward the reinforced hull plates of Vanguard Station in a seemingly poorly controlled spin was exactly what she had planned at this point.

***

"Well done, Clarice."

The captain grinned. If they'd aimed for anywhere but the docking port on purpose, they'd get shot at—they'd almost gotten shot at anyway, but they now appeared to be entirely out of control and didn't look like a threat. If they actually crashed headfirst into the station, they'd hardly make a dent, but their ship would flatten and break apart. Nobody on the station worried about that. The earlier weapons lock was a precaution in case of a suicide attack. The captain trusted Morgan would not let it be a suicide run.

Zo was in one of the cargo bays, headed for the airlock, held in place only by her heavy-duty mag boots as the ship spun. She grabbed her gear, getting ready to exit, and motioned for Jonas, who was there with her, to be ready.

"You ready to go?"

"I'm always ready, Captain, you know that."

Jonas held up his thumb. He was perhaps the most optimistic person in the crew. Zo nodded back at him.

"Good . . . Stay ready. We have a margin of error of a couple of seconds at most."

***

"Vanguard, we're pulsing retro-thrusters now. We think we may be able to change course enough to avoid a crash. 3. 2. 1. Firing."

The thrusters roared and shook the ship as they started pulsing in a computer-controlled pattern to counteract the rotation that kept changing the direction the thrusters pointed in. They slowly shifted momentum enough that the ship was no longer going to get crushed against the reinforced bulkheads of the station. The spin stopped. They had a consistent *down* for a while.

They weren't trying to avoid a crash entirely. Trying to avoid a head-on crash, sure. The side thruster burns were carried out by a program written to adjust them subtly enough to appear believable but set them on a heading for

36

the outer rim of the cylinder, in order to let them hit the very edge with enough force to look real without putting the ship at risk.

"Clarice . . . We're still coming in too hot. Are you on it?"

Vincent wasn't usually the type to sound worried like this.

"Don't worry, Vincent, we'll live."

Clarice didn't look up; her eyes were blacked out, and her fingers moved in thin air against her gloves as she adjusted the parameters of her simulation.

The ship started scraping along the edge of the hull of Vanguard. Their cameras picked up hull plating flying. Inside, of course, they couldn't hear the impact of the hull plating they were shedding against Vanguard, but they could hear a deep rumble as the whine of metal against the outer hull plating was mediated and shifted in pitch as it passed through the inner walls and the reinforced internal plating and reverberated through the ship.

It looks good, Clarice thought to herself. *Hopefully, they won't notice the airlock door opening.*

She watched Zo and Jonas from the interior airlock camera. As confident as she was in her abilities, her palms were still sweating in her gloves and she was biting her lips, an old habit she'd thought she'd long suppressed.

When the door opened and they slipped out, she held her breath for a moment until she knew she had to react to prevent jeopardizing the mission.

***

"Sorry for that Vanguard—we appear to have scraped your paint and left some of our hull behind. We're proceeding to standard holding distance as best we can, but with nav thrusters only, it'll take us many hours to bleed our remaining speed . . . If you are able to provide assistance to haul us in for repairs that would be greatly appreciated."

Morgan tried her best to sound like she was upset and rattled over what just happened.

"This is Vanguard Control. We half expected to have to smear you off our hull. Happy to see you're still alive. Hold for tugboats. You will, of course, be fined for this, and you will subject yourselves to a full inquiry."

37

The voice was stern and cold, but not hostile. They were being told off, not threatened.

"Crystal clear, Vanguard. Our apologies again. *Black Rain* out."

Once Vanguard C&C were off radio, the crew's focus instantly shifted.

"Are Jonas and the cap okay?"

Morgan was facing Vincent, who was going over their recordings of the near crash.

Vincent Boer was ex-military, ex-mercenary, and the ship's weapons officer as well as cook, as much as anyone had clear roles in a crew this small. He'd fought colonist insurgents in six colonies before he started thinking maybe the other side was right, and *retired* to the *Black Rain* for what he considered a nice relaxing job where getting shot at was only a possibility rather than a certainty on any given day.

"Don't know . . ." answered Vincent, turning towards her. "Damn thing is spinning at nearly 340 km/h—they were out of view too quickly to tell."

It was the only time Clarice had seen Vincent worried, and it gave her chills.

Chapter 6

Jonas and Zo jumped out the cargo door and fired their suit thrusters briefly to get out of the way of *Black Rain* as the ship continued its faked tumble.

They got clear of the ship but now the rim of Vanguard was flying past them at high speed.

"Quick. Fire!" Zo yelled over the low-powered radio link.

It was essential they managed to attach to the station at the same time, and they both fired their grapple guns near simultaneously.

The mag-grips on the end attached to the hull as the outer rim of Vanguard spun past. The trajectory of their ship had only countered a tiny part of the speed of Vanguard's spin, and the station was racing past fast enough that if they hit it, they'd get shredded as if thrown at high speed onto the ground from a moving car for a second, only to get bounced back out from the station again at high speed in entirely the wrong direction.

Not that it'd matter, as they'd be dead—they'd have no way of getting back in fast enough.

They used a long cord with a lot of slack to reduce the force that would be applied when the cord went taut, with their grapple guns and cord attached to the equipment crate and to harnesses on their suits to spread out the force.

But they were still flung outwards from the station by the centrifugal force, like a stone on a string, hanging *below* the rim. Jonas had used mag-grips many times before, but he'd never applied this kind of force to them, and he held his breath even though he knew what they were rated for.

Being flung outward made him feel nauseated, and the cord stretched and he slowed, briefly closed his eyes, and put all his focus into not vomiting.

He was briefly flung inwards again, before his movement slowed, and he desperately looked around for Zo, confused about which direction to look in.

She looked shaken too, but was hanging not many meters away, along with their equipment crate.

They quickly engaged the motor attached to the equipment crate to help them ascend the ropes up to the rim of Vanguard, and attached additional mag-grips to hold them in place more securely.

As far as they could tell, they'd *landed* far enough from where *Black Rain* scratched along the surface to be out of sight of any maintenance crews or drones sent to inspect the damage.

Zo started unfurling the breaching kit, and Jonas began connecting it. They worked fast and in silence. Both had practiced this many times while they prepared.

If this had been war, and they'd been military, they'd be arriving in a breaching pod that'd slam anchors into the hull, attach and pull up automatically, and start cutting and burning through the hull plating.

Fast and brutal. Designed to get you in before the force inside could get to wherever you attached.

But they were not military, and a military-grade breaching pod was big, noisy, and easy to detect, relying on the expectation that any station would detect a big lump of mass thrown at it from a known attacker, so subtlety was pointless.

As it was, they hoped the confusion around the crash would mean nobody was looking for two people and a small crate hanging from the rim like this, or worst case, if they were detected, would assume it was just debris and not worry about it until it was too late and they were inside.

Their breaching kit was small, and annoyingly slow to use, but had the benefit of stealth.

It attached with a few small mag-grips similar to the grips you would use to get a suitable hand-grip on a hull for maintenance, spread out and interconnected. Weak enough not to trigger any sensors, as otherwise the alarms would go off or have to account for every maintenance crew.

It was effectively a small tent similar to those used by mountain climbers halfway up a mountain, but without a roof.

Zo meticulously sealed the sides to the hull with suction strips and a sealant.

It'd leak over time, but slow enough not to be a concern. It needed to prevent the hole they were about to open from causing a rapid loss of air pressure that'd trigger life support alarms inside the station, so it needed to stick; but once inside they'd seal it further.

Jonas was getting their tools out slowly and carefully—they couldn't afford a wrong move. If they sliced open their *tent* they would quickly be in trouble, and they hardly had any space to move in and kept brushing up against each other.

Jonas Borgen was a former martial arts champion who one day decided that with the Earth-Centauri gate opening coming up, he wanted to work in space. Get into a position so that when the gate opened, he'd have a chance to get a job on one of the ships due to leave Sol. He wanted adventure. To see the galaxy. He'd spent ten years hauling cargo in near-Earth space before signing on with the captain. But he'd also spent a lot of that time learning to adapt his fighting style to different gravity, and staying in shape.

His flexibility and low gravity experience came in handy for missions like this, but it was still a challenge to do this work without ending up hurting each other.

They used a pair of small, low-power plasma welders to let them slowly cut through the hull plating. They had to work slowly, letting the surrounding plating regularly cool both for their own survival, given the tight space, and to avoid a large enough heat build-up to trigger fire alarms or other sensors. As long as they moved slow enough, it'd stay below the tolerances once again added to avoid triggering alarms for every maintenance crew.

"Watch it."

"Sorry, Cap."

Jonas had almost put the welder against Zo's helmet. It would have cut through her faceplate in seconds. They needed to stay focused during every second as they worked their way along the inside edge of the breaching kit.

"Shit. I think we have a hole."

There was a noticeable current of air escaping the hole they had started opening.

Jonas grabbed an aerosol canister and sprayed. It sprayed a light dust of particles. Lit by their suit lamps, they could see the particles moved by the current of air towards a corner of the kit where the seal was not holding.

41

Zo brought out more sealant and applied it to the corner, and the stream stopped.

"Should be okay now."

Jonas looked over the repair. It seemed solid, and the air currents had reduced to the chaos from their own movements one could expect in a mostly closed space.

"Let's check again regularly."

They returned to the plasma welders.

Chapter 7

They had estimated about two hours to cut through Vanguard's outermost walls.

It took three before they had a hole big enough for both of them to fit through and into the outer maintenance tunnels.

"You okay?" Jonas asked, getting his helmet off first.

"Yeah, just feeling like I've been boiled in my suit."

They were both dripping with sweat after the work and the heat from the welding equipment.

The tunnels would be too narrow to keep the EVA gear on, so they stripped that off immediately inside and put on generic work suits from their equipment bags that would hopefully be close enough to the station work suits to not draw attention if they were spotted.

They had to empty the weapons and tools they were smuggling out of their crate into two heavy bags.

"I'll close up the tent, you finish packing the bags."

Zo closed up the *roof* of the tent and triggered a small pump that deflated it. She used a canister of specialized expanding sealant with a composition similar to a mix of quick-setting concrete and adhesive that was pumped into the tent to glue the deflated tent together and to the hull. The space-station equivalent of a tire patch. It would hold well enough until someone in maintenance would get mighty pissed off when they eventually noticed the source of what would almost certainly, over time, develop into a slow, steady leak. To remove it and weld the hole properly would be a cumbersome and dangerous job.

"All done with the bags, Cap. I gave you all the heavy gear."

Jonas always made his jokes in the driest, most deadpan way possible—people who didn't know him could never tell if he was joking or not.

Zo lifted her bag and shook it as if to assess the weight.

"I can tell." She smiled.

43

Jonas noted with some relief that they'd avoided the section that held the station sewage treatment plant. They'd entered a section holding one of the hydroponics bays. It was dim, with specialized LEDs above each growth chamber that minimized the light emitted to just the wavelengths most effective for the various types of plants to keep energy usage down. The paths in between were cramped.

"This direction, I think." Zo led the way.

They made their way to one of the doorways and exited into one of the larger hallways.

The air was still hot and humid—these hydroponics bays, like the sewage plant, were used as convenient heat sinks and buffers because the heat was useful here, and even though they were nowhere near the sewage plant, there was still a pressing smell somewhat like manure from the growth-mediums in the bays.

They could practically taste the earthy smell as they slowly moved through the hallway, carefully listening in case they ran into any maintenance workers, but they met none.

They got to the nearest lift and checked it, but it required access passes which they did not have. They kept walking and found a ventilation shaft just a little bit further down.

Jonas leaned in and looked up, and had Zo take a look as well.

"What do you think, Zo?"

"It's probably our best option. It's wide enough. I think we can make it."

"I'll get the equipment out."

The shaft had steps built into one side for maintenance crews to climb, but climbing it with their heavy equipment bags would be too slow and grueling.

It was the worst part of the station to be climbing in, with the simulated gravity close to earth standard.

Jonas brought out mag-grips with a small motorized pulley to help speed the climb significantly. They would have to stretch up, put one grip in place, then let the motor-assist help haul the bags up while they climbed.

"Okay, all good."

Jonas attached the first grips and started climbing. Zo would detach the ones furthest down as she followed.

It was still exhausting and slow, and they had around two hundred meters, or six hundred feet, to get to the station's inner *floor*. They hoped they wouldn't have to climb the ventilation shaft the whole way—the thought made Jonas queasy.

"Shh . . ."

They were a few floors up when sudden light from above made Jonas signal to Zo to stop and be quiet. They stayed tense while trying to calm their breathing. Somebody made the metal clang loudly, as though he was working on something. After a couple of minutes, Jonas motioned for Zo, and they slowly pulled themselves up to an access hatch about two meters above, still well below where the man was.

"Think we can get it open without him noticing us?" Zo whispered.

"I think we need to try. We're too exposed here."

Jonas tried to open the hatch as quietly as he could. He didn't notice any sounds, but the man above went quiet, and Jonas worried he might have heard.

Soon, the man went back to working and they crawled inside. It was even darker inside the hatch, and they waited until the man started packing up.

The man left, but seconds later a door opened behind them, dim lights came on, and they realized the hatch they'd climbed into was on a short access tunnel attached to a stairwell, and the man from before was coming down toward them. They weren't sure whether or not he'd be able to see them.

They sunk further into the shadows and hoped he'd pass. The man stopped at their floor, opened an access hatch on the opposite side of where they'd climbed in, and crawled inside without looking in their direction.

Luckily for him—the captain had her stun gun out and was ready to use it to prevent any alarms being raised. Instead, they managed to sneak past him and up the stairs.

They got up eight floors that way before they hit a door that again required an access card.

"We should have taken him out after all and taken his pass," Jonas grumbled.

"But then security would be alerted when he came to," the captain pointed out.

"I guess you're right."

Jonas knew she was right, but was still unhappy about it. If they wanted to take his card, they'd have had to spend time finding somewhere to hide him—dead or alive—long enough to carry out their job or they'd risk having security scouring the station.

They found another access hatch and crawled back into the ventilation shaft, and started climbing up again. This time, Zo was first. They were soon exhausted and dripping in sweat again, though thankfully the temperature was dropping as they got higher.

Eventually, they reached another hatch, and this time they were lucky—they found a staircase where the upper door didn't require an access card.

"Hold back. I'll check if it is safe."

Jonas stuck his head out to see where they were and look for any guards. He was about to signal for Zo to follow when he quickly pulled his head back in, and crouched down, quietly closing the door.

"What's wrong?"

"A guard. I don't think he saw me."

The armed guard walked up the corridor and, from the sound of it, passed right by the door, and then it went quiet.

Jonas was not sure if he'd rounded the corner in the other direction, or if he'd stopped. Or maybe the guard *had* spotted him and was waiting for him to show himself.

They waited several minutes and when there was no further sound, Jonas looked out again.

The corridor was empty, and they quickly slid out the door. They tried to walk as normally as possible, pretending to be ordinary workers, but they needed to determine which floor they were on and find their way. They could not risk running into anyone before they were sure they were off any staff-only floors where they'd likely be asked for ID.

They peered around the corner and saw an information terminal. Unfortunately, there was also a guard standing there.

Chapter 8

The Vanguard tugboat intercepted them as their nav thrusters were still working hard to slow them down. It matched their speed and alignment carefully, and a couple of the tugboat crew went outside to help them attach cables to haul them.

Grant and Mons joined the Vanguard staff outside to help attach the cables to help accelerate them to a somewhat more decent speed than they'd achieve with the nav thrusters alone, so it wouldn't take them too long to get back. The cables were long, and the Vanguard crew boosted toward the *Black Rain* using suit thrusters, pulling the thick cables with them.

It would still take them hours to get back, as they were constrained both by the strength of the cables and by the complexity and risk involved in separation. Pulling a spacecraft this way was more akin to trying to pull a heavy load on ice than in water, except in three dimensions instead of two. Most importantly, once you set the load in motion, it won't stop by itself once you stop pulling.

***

"Tugboat, this is *Black Rain*, we're ready when you are."

Clarice was bored. They'd spend several hours on this exercise, though it was still far better than letting the nav thrusters do the whole job. She wished she hadn't needed to intentionally damage the main engine intentionally to make things look good. Pretending they'd fixed it would make the flight back so much faster, but it'd be hard to explain.

The acceleration was still gentle, though much faster than their nav thrusters allowed. It took them two hours to get to the halfway point.

The tugboat slowed slightly, and the locks on the *Black Rain's* side of the cables unlocked to release them. Clarice watched on the cameras as the cables were winched in.

"Everyone ready to flip."

Clarice confirmed everyone was strapped in and used the nav thrusters to turn the ship for deceleration.

She observed on the monitors as the tug circled around them and lined up to repeat the maneuver again, and gave the okay for Grant and Mons to prep to help again.

At their current speed, they'd crash straight into Vanguard's docking port, and they needed the tug's help to slow down as well.

***

"Vanguard, we're ready to dock . . . Finally."

"Good to see you again, *Black Rain*. How was the trip?"

"Ha, ha. Very funny, Vanguard." Clarice was even more annoyed than she sounded.

"Please proceed to bay C."

The docking bays on Vanguard were arranged as one huge entrance area that set the limit for the largest ships the station could accommodate, which led to a space where you were effectively at the top of six separate landing bays arranged as a hexagon about ⅓ of the distance toward where the outer hull of the main station was.

They matched the station rotation, entered, and finally rotated the ship to match the prescribed bay as ordered, before they carefully descended using the nav thrusters only. It wouldn't cause a problem—the perceived gravity in the landing bays was minor.

"So, what do you think the odds are we'll be thrown in a cell?" Vincent didn't seem to be seriously concerned about it, as he was grinning.

"We'll find out soon. I think we were convincing enough, so hopefully it'll just be a stern talking-to."

Clarice locked down the bridge controls, and as the two last ones off the ship, they headed to the exit.

There was a security contingent waiting for them. They walked through the normal weapons scans with no incidents, then they were escorted in from the docking area to the main station, and down several floors. The security office had enough of a feeling of gravity that their mag-shoes adjusted down to almost no grip.

"Here they are, sir."

"This is Lieutenant Xavier Smyth. He'll take it from here."

Two of the security guards that accompanied them turned and left. The one who was speaking remained.

"Thank you." Mr. Smyth spoke with few hints of emotion. He was a heavy-set man, but quite tall, wearing a uniform that didn't quite fit. He wore thick-rimmed round glasses with lenses that seemed too small for his face.

"Ms. Morgan? Follow me."

Smyth's tone was sharp, and he made no sign of wanting to shake her hand or looking back to see if she did, in fact, follow him to the interview room.

The rest waited as Clarice got up and followed. She thought it was a good sign that only one guard was made to stay in the security office where the others were made to wait.

"Sit, Ms. Morgan."

Lt. Smyth pointed to a chair in the sparsely decorated room. Clarice had been in interrogation rooms before. This looked exactly the same as anywhere else.

If the man had any feelings about the incident, his face didn't show it. His expression showed a mild interest, but no hint of anger.

"We got very close to deciding to blow you to pieces out there . . . Ms. Morgan."

He adjusted his glasses slightly.

"It says here you're the first officer. Where is your captain?"

"The captain is spending a week recuperating, sir."

"Nothing serious, I hope?"

"Too many parties, too little time, sir."

Clarice disliked authority, and hated having to be deferential to station security, but being an asshole to him would just cause unwanted attention, so she forced herself to joke and smile and call him *sir* without too much noticeable sarcasm.

"And you've decided to take the ship for a spin while she's 'indisposed'?"

49

Smyth looked up at her briefly, with only the slightest lift in the corners of his mouth hinting that he was making a joke and trying to suppress a smile.

"Captain's orders, sir. As documented in the ship's log. We passed the documentation to your systems prior to our accident. A client wanted us to pick up a small shipment of radioactives from the belt, and wasn't in the mood to wait, and the captain was in even less of a mood to lose the income."

" . . . Sir."

"Ah, yes. I see. And your licenses appear to be in order. Including your insurance; fortunately for both of us, but mostly for you. But if you're getting radioactives from the belt, why are you here?"

"We were low on helium-3, and as you know, helium-3 is substantially cheaper here than on Earth."

Smyth gave her a stiff smile that didn't seem very genuine and flipped through a few more pages on his tablet.

They'd picked up helium-3 in moon orbit before. It was a common thing to do, so Clarice was not worried.

***

As he looked through the documents, Smyth looked less and less interested.

It was late in his shift, and exciting as it had been to consider whether or not the ship would end up getting crushed against the Vanguard's rather substantially more solid hull—an excitement Smyth was not particularly proud of but that was there anyway—that excitement had turned to dull disinterest and then boredom once they'd all survived and it became clear there was going to be a lot of paperwork.

"Our engineers say the engine malfunction appears to be due to a short in engine control that burned out a control board. Easily fixed apparently, and our maintenance crew indicates you did minimal damage. Says you just missed one of our communications towers. Good for you, those things are expensive and take lots of work to replace, and you'd have found us far more cranky."

He flipped a page.

"Everything seems to indicate your crew did all they could to deflect, everyone has passed their drug screens, and I am not in the mood for a lot of paperwork. You may go, Ms. Morgan. Be more careful next time—you might not always catch me in this mood."

He looked up at her with a tired expression on his face and motioned to the guard at the door.

"Enjoy your stay."

"Thank you, sir." Morgan smiled briefly at the officer and walked out.

***

"Sir?"

Lt. Smyth turned around slowly.

"Yes?"

A young sergeant stood by his door and handed him a pad. Smyth looked over it, quickly flipping the pages.

"We're still inspecting the footage. But nothing unusual to report so far, sir."

The officer waited while Smyth went through the rest of the data and handed the pad back. He looked unsure as to what to do afterwards, but remained in position.

Something still didn't add up for Lt. Smyth.

When he started on the paperwork after interviewing Ms. Morgan, it had struck him that something about it felt too neat. What were the odds they'd manage to hit the station so precisely on the rim, rather than slamming into it?

He had checked—there'd been a handful of crashes into Vanguard over the years. They'd all tried to avoid the station, but ended up crashing while desperately trying to veer off. They'd all partially rotated. They'd hit the station at different locations.

There were also about a dozen who had been about to hit, but managed to get clear.

But grazing the rim the way they did, meant not managing to turn the ship away much, given the 1 km radius of Vanguard. That hadn't happened before.

"Have someone keep an eye on the *Black Rain* crew."

"Right away, sir."

"Oh, and have a guard posted near the ship."

Chapter 9

Jonas pulled his head back and motioned for Zo to be quiet and pull back too.

"There's an information terminal there, but a guard is hanging around it."

"Let's see if he'll leave first."

They moved up to the corner and waited for several minutes, but the guard made no sign of moving.

They were too exposed if someone came from behind, so decided to risk it.

"Wait here with the bags. Keep your weapon ready."

She straightened up, wiped her brow, and strode out.

"Hey! I seem to be lost."

She smiled at the guard, who looked surprised to see her.

"I don't know if I'm even meant to be here . . . I got on a lift and was meant to get off at the lower hab levels, but some station staff got on and I clearly need sleep because I didn't pay attention to the floors."

Zo walked close to the guard, who clutched his plasma rifle, but didn't show any sign of lifting it.

"You're a couple of levels too far down, ma'am. You're not really meant to be here."

He looked her up and down.

"I'm so sorry." Zo wasn't a great actor but the guard didn't seem to notice.

"It's okay, it's not restricted or anything. Here, I'll show you where to go."

He turned and started walking toward Jonas. Zo walked with him and tried to distract him by asking his name and if he'd worked at Vanguard long.

When they rounded the corner, she was relieved to see Jonas had had enough time to manage to hide. The guard led her further down in the other direction and through a doorway to the lift banks.

"Here, you see. The hab levels are this bank labeled E."

The guard swiped his access card and pointed at the lift display for her, and she thanked him and got in. He waited for her to pick a level, and the door to close. She had to find a way back down to Jonas afterward, conscious she'd be unable to get the lift back down to this level without a card. She hoped he had the good sense to stay where he was.

She got out on the lowest hab level, just three floors above where she got on. At least that was good news. She tried her radio to see if she could reach Jonas or Clarice. She got through to Clarice, though with a very poor connection.

"Hey, where are you?"

"I'm at the lowest hab level, but Jonas is stuck three levels below. I tried reaching him but it's still too well shielded."

"We're four levels above you. We've got a cabin for you to wait in. Do you need help?"

"No, we should be okay. Don't risk anything. Send me the room codes. We'll be in touch."

Zo got back in the lift and tried the floor they'd been on just in case, but as expected, it prompted for a key card. She expected she'd have to find another route, but the lift started going up. Instead of trying to get off as soon as possible, she decided to wait it out and see if she'd be lucky enough to get staff come on. The lift went up to the top hab level and four people got on. Two were clearly visitors and pressed floors lower in the hab levels. The last person was a woman that swiped a staff pass and picked a floor in the section she was headed to but further down. Zo saw her chance and asked if she'd press her floor: F3. The woman glanced at her poking out from behind the two others and obliged.

Zo hoped she wouldn't subject her to more scrutiny once the two others left, and got lucky—more staff got on and the lift was full. One of them carelessly put their card in their left pocket and Zo, as carefully as she could, lifted it out.

Once they got to F3, Zo squeezed past the other staff and the woman who'd pressed her floor quickly and quietly, while holding on to the swiped staff pass.

She made her way back up the corridor to find Jonas, conscious she'd need to be careful not to run into the same guard again.

"Zo, here."

Jonas had snuck back into the stairwell to wait.

"I was just about to give up waiting and look for another route up."

Zo flashed him the staff pass.

"We need to hurry. The person I lifted it off will undoubtedly miss it quickly."

They didn't want to risk running in case anyone saw them, but they carried the tool bags as rapidly as they could while trying to appear as if they were just going about their business.

They got to the elevator bank and swiped the access card. Soon they were back up at the habitation levels, this time on the floor where Clarice had arranged for them to have a room. Zo tried to contact Clarice on the radio again and was able to get in touch.

"I got Jonas. We will head for the room you booked and stay there. We'll meet at night as arranged."

"Great. See you then. Be careful."

Clarice sounded distinctly relieved.

Jonas and Zo headed straight for the room and found it easily. It was small and cramped as hotel rooms go, but for a space station it wasn't bad, and they were both used to the cramped quarters of a space ship.

Though, most of the time on the *Black Rain* they could roam freely about the ship, and when in zero-g they could use all the surfaces. Here, they were limited to a single floor.

But all they really wanted was an opportunity to clean up and rest before the mission later that evening.

Zo offered Jonas the bathroom first and sat down to go through the plans one last time.

Chapter 10

Vanguard was the first of its kind—the first station built for a large contingent of permanent residents, and it was considered a failure on that count.

While parts of the station, such as the storage floors, were lit 24/7, the *surface*—the inner tubular open space that passed for outside of sorts, and any buildings protruding into it—observed a simulated day/night cycle to create the illusion of an open space.

Most of the living quarters—the more expensive ones, anyway—were located there, pretending to be houses in a weird little town where in one direction you could walk about five kilometers and be back where you started, while in the other direction it was roughly five kilometers to get from the main entrances from the public docking area to the private docks on the other end of the station.

In the middle, a cylinder with a radius of just about a hundred meters jutted out of the docking section and stretched from one end-cap to the other. One third of the way in from either side, it met four massive spokes set evenly around the cylinder to reinforce the structure and provide elevator and utility shafts.

This center spire held Command and Control and, on the exterior, there were a series of massive lights that served to simulate day and night, creating an illusion of a string of tiny suns during the day. It was painted Earth-sky blue so that having its bulk obscure the ground that was *straight down* from one's perspective, was meant to give somewhat of an illusion of a sky, though somewhat diminished by the string of light and a number of visible windows. This never really gave the intended effect in any case, as the spire was too narrow to obscure enough of the opposite side of the cylinder.

Someone who arrived without having seen a major space station before would quickly get disoriented—looking near where you stood was like being at the bottom of a relatively gently sloping valley, but if you let your eyes follow the curve, and lifted your gaze even a little, there was nothing resembling open sky, and you'd easily feel like you were hanging from a ceiling looking down from a building hundreds of floor up.

This was the reason it was considered a failure.

It wasn't unusual for first-time visitors to get panic attacks, and some people avoided the floor level as much as they could, opting for the large basement malls.

The far bigger Vanguard II solved this with scale. Smaller stations solved this by not trying for this kind of ambitious simulated open space.

As an artifact of its military origin, shock absorbers on the spokes and where the spire met the docking complexes ensured the station could be hit by massive barrages without affecting C&C, which, in effect, sat suspended in the middle, floating as a station inside the station.

Very limited physical access options meant even a full breach would leave an invading force a hard time approaching, without becoming targets for sentry guns, their computer systems largely under continued control from C&C.

Central control systems were tied to C&C via redundant conduits through the spokes, as well as through the center spire, and via encrypted radio links to multiple points throughout the station. This meant that until an invader had a chance to either blow up C&C, or take out all ten wired connections and the wireless receivers, anyone in C&C with sufficient clearance could disable life support for whole sections or even vent atmosphere for the entire station, except for the self-contained air supply in C&C.

They could also make use of any still functioning communication arrays to ask for help, or blow the whole thing up by forcibly overloading the reactors running the place. Adding to that, if an invader managed to shut down the links before taking out at least half a dozen systems, various station systems would automatically assume an attack and take countermeasures ranging from sealing internal bulkheads, venting non-habitation modules, and triggering distress beacons.

Vanguard's military past meant it was unusually well protected against a takeover, and unusually prepared to sacrifice life in the process. Even more so if required in order to deny an invader a victory.

There were secondary control stations in both end-caps in case primary C&C became totally inoperable, but the point of placing C&C in the center rather than in the end caps was that, in a military station during a conflict, you don't expect to survive long if you place C&C where attacking crafts can see it and slam big, heavy and/or explosive stuff into you.

The secondary C&Cs were there for cases where you were pretty much dead anyway: electricity gone, or image feeds from the hull busted. You'd be able to stare out at the destruction headed your way, but not likely be able to do much. But at least you could try.

To take over primary C&C with a large scale assault, an army would have to first fight their way through the lower decks or the heavily reinforced docking stations, then manage to get enough weapons in place for a large scale assault on the spire without the people there noticing and disabling the air supply, enabling sentry guns and/or blowing up the station.

More importantly for the mission, in the same spire was the central vault of the station. It wasn't a big vault. Other vaults for commercial use and most station use were spread throughout the station and handled the majority of needs. The central vault was small and mostly used for official purposes. It was not in itself particularly well protected—the difficulty of breaching it was all down to location.

They clearly wouldn't survive a full frontal assault, so they were entirely dependent on stealth. If they wanted to steal the canister without entering the well-guarded docking ring, which seemed particularly foolish to attempt, they would need to get up to the central spire without attracting attention too soon. However, the only way of doing so would be to go *outside*, which didn't exactly make for an easy assault either.

Chapter 11

The crew, except for Zo and Jonas, were waiting for station local night, which would be their opportunity.

It would still be high risk, but at least there would be fewer people around and they had a reasonable shot at not being spotted too early.

The group found a diner and sat down for a light dinner while waiting for evening. They carefully avoided talking about anything related to the mission. Afterward, they milled around a bit until the lights gradually started dimming to simulate twilight, while they were trying to act as normal as possible.

They went back to the rooms they'd hired, with food for Jonas and the captain, who wanted to avoid being seen in public in case they ran into security who might run their details against the station manifest and discover they weren't officially on the station.

As soon as it was dark enough, they got ready to leave.

They all changed into clothes that were plausible yet dark to reduce their chance of being spotted against the military gray of the spokes. They *borrowed* some dustbins to hide their equipment and weapons in.

Clarice's eyes had a faint red glow signaling she'd switched on her infrared filter. The glow was artificial and could be turned off, but she quite liked how unsettled it seemed to make people to see her eyes colored red like embers of a fire.

She smiled to herself, trying to hide that she was nervous. She did not often go out in the field, and very rarely on operations that would likely involve fire-fights.

But she wasn't going to let anyone see. She turned up the brightness of the red light in her eyes a little, hoping she'd look more scary than nervous.

They made their way through the walkways to a small park surrounding one of the spokes slowly and carefully. During the day, they had intentionally avoided going near the spokes, as while there were public spaces surrounding them, there were also usually guards there, and they had worried about drawing attention.

Jonas grabbed a chain from his bag, and wrapped it around the gates leading into the park, and locked it up with a padlock. He placed a sufficiently official-looking sign they had printed out for the occasion, before they found a secluded spot right next to the spoke and started preparing their gear.

Most of their gear was relatively innocent climbing gear that consisted of grappling hooks, freshly charged mag-grips, and synthetic ropes.

But they'd also brought a number of weapons, most of which were sufficiently powerful that they were either illegal or would have had to be declared and locked down in the station armory for the duration of their stay. Mostly non-lethal stun guns, but the equipment also included a number of explosives.

The climb up the spoke toward the spire wouldn't be that hard. While the station simulated 80% of Earth gravity on the *surface* through rotation, it would drop off rapidly over the seven hundred meters before they'd reach the center—at the spire, the perceived gravity was half of what it'd be on the moon's surface.

The mag-grips provided solid grips as well as decent footholds, and they'd be attached to their individual grips by rope. Though it took a lot of practice to disable and enable the electro-magnets at exactly the right moment to get a good rhythm going. Their main concern wasn't exhaustion, but detection. The station was dark, but not pitch black.

"It's weird . . . Feels like being out in moonlight, but then you look up at that weird strip of light," Vincent whispered, but Vincent whispering still felt like it was booming through the quiet night.

"I know. I keep thinking about how big the moon should be in the sky, given how close to the moon we're orbiting, and then we can't even see it because it's flying past outside the *floor.*"

Clarice briefly looked at her feet, as if her augmented eyes would let her see the moon fly past.

"Ever read *Journey to the Center of the Earth*? One of my favorite books as a kid. Vanguard kinda feels like how I pictured some of those caves . . . If they had buildings in them."

They were quickly and efficiently unpacking and distributing the equipment and weapons.

"I know what you mean," Clarice told Vincent as she started looking around, using her augmented eyesight to look out for any stragglers left in the park, or any signs of security.

She thought she heard a rustle, and went to check, but there was nobody there. She checked if Jonas had locked the door properly. He had. The *closed for maintenance* sign had fallen over. She put it back up.

Everyone was almost geared up when Clarice caught a movement in the dark behind Jonas. She had her augments replace the infrared capture, and there was definitively someone there in the bushes.

She quietly reached for her knife, and gave a quiet signal to Jonas, motioning to the bushes. She walked over to Rob, who was standing at a diagonal from where she'd seen the movement, while Jonas casually moved in the other direction, back toward the bushes, and grabbed one of the plasma torches.

"Hey, Rob."

Clarice didn't actually look at him, even though her eyes were directed straight at him.

"Don't look around you. I'm not actually looking at you," she whispered. "Just pretend we're talking."

She had rotated her vision toward the right edge of her eyes, so she was still looking at the bushes where she'd heard the sound.

"What do you want me to say?"

"Doesn't matter, I can't focus on conversation right now, there's someone in the bushes, just pretend."

A slight motion.

"Okay, I guess I'll just say random stuff then."

"*Mm-hm . . .*"

She made a hand gesture to Jonas to point him at the right bush, and Jonas quickly, and surprisingly silently, slipped behind one of the other bushes and tried to get behind whoever was hiding there.

"You still need me to talk, don't you?"

Clarice just put her finger to her mouth and slipped away from Rob to go around the other side. Just as she did, a man in a Vanguard security uniform tried to sneak out of the bush she'd been watching.

61

Without a word, he started raising his plasma gun, but he spun around when Jonas lunged for him from behind.

He got off a shot. Jonas didn't stop, and punched the man in the gut, before falling over.

Clarice stepped forward and jabbed at the man with her knife, but he stepped aside.

Just as he raised his gun again towards Clarice, Jonas grabbed the man's ankles and pulled. The shot went up until the brief flash of plasma dissipated in the air.

The others came running, but the man was already subdued; knocked unconscious against the stone slab when he fell. They tied him up and hid him in the bushes.

"You think he was alone?" Zo looked toward Clarice, then to Jonas.

"I think so, but we better check."

"What about alarms?" asked Grant.

"Nobody seems to be trying to contact him. And nobody rushing here as far as we can tell. I think we're good. Not much we can do about it if not." Jonas' voice was strained. His burn was minor, but clearly painful.

Rob was dressing the burn while Jonas was speaking, and it clearly didn't make it any easier.

"Are you sure you'll be okay, Jonas?" Zo looked worried.

"Yeah, I'll manage." Jonas forced a strained smile.

"Clarice, Vincent, check to see if anyone else is lurking around, just in case."

Clarice left the others waiting silently for a few minutes as she, accompanied by Jonas, snuck around the park and used her night sight to look for anyone else.

"Didn't see anything. But I'm sure they'll eventually notice he's missing."

Shortly after, they were finally ready to start the climb.

Chapter 12

As they started the climb, all they could do was to hope nobody would be out on a night-time walk and look too carefully, or there was a good chance they might be spotted.

Vincent and Morgan waited below for a few minutes, hidden in the bushes, in case they needed to provide covering fire. Vincent wore a pair of light night vision goggles, but Vincent knew Morgan's eyes were far superior—she'd shown him a video dump once. He wondered how much it had cost her to get them, minus the value of her real eyes. Tearing out healthy eyes like she had, freaked him out, but he was also curious how much of the bill for her replacements had been covered by selling her biological ones.

As the others had made it about fifty meters up, they were hard enough to spot that Vincent motioned for Morgan to start climbing. He followed soon after, while Jonas held in position above them, looking for movement, prepared to cover them from up there if necessary.

The first few *steps* they hauled themselves up with the help of the rope attached to a harness and the mag-grips, without proper foot support. It was hard, but they didn't want to leave any grips behind at eye height. Jonas had left a rope and pulley hanging down from a couple of stories up for Morgan and Vincent to use.

Vincent didn't like heights, but he was disciplined and knew to keep his mind focused on each step and his eyes focused close on the spoke. He worked his way up the first fifteen meters with the help of the pulley, then firmly attached a couple of mag-grips and detached the pulley and attached it to his bag—it was too visible to leave behind.

From that point it was easier—the captain, who was in the lead with Mons, had left mag-grips behind for those following to use as steps. They still moved the hand grips—the grips were tied to a rope connected to their harnesses, so as long as one of the grips remained secure, they should not be able to fall.

Vincent admired the captain. Through years as a mercenary, he'd met only a handful of people as physically tough as Zo. She was small compared to him, but muscular and flexible. He'd met even fewer people he trusted in combat as much.

He soon got into the rhythm of the climb. Disable a mag-grip. Move it up carefully, ensuring the rope did not tangle. Attach. Step up. Disable the other mag-grip. Repeat.

He was less sure about Mons. He was pleasant enough to talk to, but he was new and Vincent didn't like new. He also seemed to try a bit too hard for Vincent's liking—Vincent appreciated the chain of command and he obeyed the captain without question, but he wasn't submissive; he spoke frankly when he had an opinion. Mons, on the other hand, seemed to try very hard never to disagree with the captain.

On the upside, he didn't talk very much. Vincent liked people who didn't talk very much.

He quickly caught up to Morgan, and shortly afterward they were right below Jonas and they all formed a tight line. Every step made the next easier. By the mid-point, perceived gravity was somewhere around half a g.

Suddenly, he heard a weak whistling sound that perplexed him for a moment until he realized it was the sound of something falling. He looked up. A mag-grip was dropping straight toward him. He just about twisted his shoulder out of the way, but it bumped against his chest and Vincent took in air sharply. He barely managed to avoid letting out any sound.

Below, he could hear a relatively muted sound as the grip bounced on the grass in the park.

One of the crew above him seemed to have accidentally hit the release on one of the grips left behind.

Vincent, for a moment, felt a slight resentment at doing this job with a group that—apart from the captain and Grant—to his mind, were amateurs when it came to what Vincent saw as a combat op.

Cap might think we'll be able to do this with minimal fighting, he thought to himself, *but it won't take many little noises like that before one of them gets heard, and we're in a full fire-fight.*

Vincent thought about the crew, and how they might do.

Jonas was an excellent close combat fighter, but he had limited field experience. Clarice's eyes were a major asset, but she was young and over-eager in a way that made Vincent feel protective, and he didn't know how she'd do with a gun. Mons seemed better suited for infiltration than combat, and Vincent imagined he'd surrender the moment someone pointed a weapon at him, though perhaps that was unfair. Rob was a good medic, but he was useless with a weapon.

Flying with them was fine, but this kept him extra on edge; he expected to have to carry several of them.

He could see the first of the group reached the spire. The captain had started the next phase. Vincent allowed himself a grin and a brief moment to watch her work her way slowly outward, admiring her methodical and disciplined progress.

While gravity was lower than the moon up there, they were on the outside, and would need to work their way out to the nearest windows, which meant hanging from the grips and their ropes, with a seven hundred meter drop. And while the perceived gravity was high enough for the drop to start slowly, they'd accelerate soon enough if they fell.

More time to contemplate their death if they were to fall, Vincent thought casually.

The captain had fixed one rope to Mons' harness, via a pulley, through one of the grip handles, and to her harness. Another rope was fixed to a grip, and she was moving slowly out along the spire, placing a grip, clipping a short rope from her harness onto it, then threading a rope through. She left grips approximately every ten meters to hold the rope in place.

After watching her briefly, Vincent continued climbing until he was bunched up with the rest of them.

***

When the captain was roughly a hundred meters out, she reached a window and peeked in. She gave a thumbs up and affixed the rope she had been threading to one of the grips, then fastened herself to two grips on the side. It made it significantly easier for the rest of them, who could hook themselves to the rope and rapidly move outward without attaching their grips every step. They just had to attach every ten meters or so to unhook and re-hook their harness to the rope every time it threaded through a grip handle.

Soon, they were all hanging around the window, ready to get in rapidly once they cut it open.

C&C itself was located in a somewhat bulbous section in the middle, with the vault and a few other higher security areas immediately adjacent. The section they were about to enter contained staff recreation areas and maintenance.

They would have a very short window of time to get inside and seek cover if they wanted to be sure not to get seen and have all hell break loose.

Luckily station regulations on weapons had the beneficial side-effect that regular station security would be lightly armed, as they didn't have reason to expect to meet armed resistance without warning. Especially not in the spire itself. There was an armory, but if they were spotted, it'd take several minutes before they'd be facing more heavily armed resistance.

A massive crashing sound tore through the station, and everything shook. The spire was relatively protected by the extensive suspension, but it still shook.

Vincent looked around, his first instinct to account for everyone. Everyone seemed okay.

Then Grant fell past him; his mag-grips had given in.

They tried reaching for each other but didn't get a grip.

He looked down and saw Grant bounce. He had still been attached to the threaded safety rope and fell just a couple of floors before he bounced as he reached the end.

Vincent almost got sick at the combination of the steep drop and seeing him bob up and down. He took a second to stare at the spire wall to compose himself before he attached an extra grip and used a clamp around Grant's rope in case any other clamps had shaken loose. He whispered for everyone to double-check their ropes and clamps, and motioned for Jonas to help him pull Grant up.

Between the low perceived gravity, Grant climbing his side of the rope, and Jonas and Vincent, they had him up and reattached to the wall within the minute.

They now felt a sense of urgency to get in, outweighing any sense of caution, and they checked the window again. With nobody in sight, the captain hit it with a plasma blast and they filed in.

The first thing Vincent heard as he climbed in the window was guards shouting and klaxons going off.

Chapter 13

"What the hell was that?"

"We're under fire!"

Vanguard C&C was in chaos. People were literally bouncing off the walls after the first hit. They were used to low-g, and quickly regained control, got back to their stations and strapped in, then started searching for the cause.

***

Zo was first in. Her first impulse was to duck and roll when inside, but the gravity was too low for that to have worked, so she resisted her impulse and kicked off hard against the inner wall as soon as she was clear of the window, and flew across the room. She caught herself and took care not to push back hard enough to fly back across the room. She grabbed hold of a ledge and turned around to assess.

There were no immediate threats, but she could hear loud voices from outside the room and she had no doubt someone must have heard something.

The others were entering and she jumped back and started helping them in, and motioned for them to ready their weapons one by one as they entered.

***

"Report." Vanguard's XO stared at his screens.

"A ship is attacking the private docking ring. Looks military. No transponder."

***

They could hear people running in the corridor now, and the sound was getting louder. While they were in the middle of getting into position, the door was flung open.

Zo was braced against the wall and fired her stun gun by pure reflex before she could even tell if someone was in the door opening. She must have hit someone as she heard a startled scream, but they were jettisoned backward by the impact and Zo couldn't see if they were disabled by her shot. She reasoned they had to be.

Vincent climbed through the window while Zo moved closer to the door.

Before she got there, Grant motioned to their masks, and threw a smoke grenade into the hallway before anyone could react to his hand motion, much less put their mask on.

Zo swore to herself. Grant was always over-eager, with an attitude to safety that seemed to involve erring on the side of more explosives. It's a wonder he'd not lost any major body parts.

She grabbed her mask and put it on. A couple of the crew were coughing, but she was unsure who, as the smoke filled the room they were in too.

Zo yelled a request for status.

"Grant can go and fuck himself!"

"Yeah, fuck you, Grant."

"Thank you. Thank you all."

Apart from a series of angry expletives hurled at Grant for throwing the smoke grenade without giving people time to get their masks on, everyone confirmed they were masked and okay.

Klaxons started blaring, and they could no longer hear whether anyone was in the corridor because of the loud noise.

***

"Sir, we have reports of an incursion into the spire. At least one down."

"How the hell did they get in? The ship just appeared on our screens seconds before they fired, and there are no indications of breaching pods."

Everyone was typing furiously, processing inbound reports to get an idea of damage. On the screens were flashes as the station was firing back at the attackers.

"Reinforcements to C&C now . . . And bring the fucking gas masks, there are attackers in the spire, and one of our teams reported gas."

69

With their masks on, Zo and Vincent took up positions on either side of the door to the hallway. Coughs from the smoke grenade barely rose over the klaxons from at least a couple of guards that hadn't pulled back.

Grant moved up next to Zo and held up a flashbang and looked at her. She nodded her agreement.

At least he asked this time, she thought to herself.

Grant threw the grenade into the hallway. The flashbangs didn't have much concussive force and wouldn't cause much permanent harm, but the light and sound were painfully intense even when it landed down the corridor with a wall separating them from the sound and the smoke diminishing the light. Screams filled the corridor afterward, as the unprepared guards had taken the full brunt of it.

Zo thought Grant looked like he was enjoying this a bit too much, as she threw herself into the hallway by pushing off against the door frame, closely followed by Vincent. They could make out three shapes and fired rapidly.

"Clear!"

They stumbled through the smoke and over bodies, and within seconds they were leaping down the corridor, to the extent they could run in a less than moon gravity aided by mag boots, trying to orient themselves as they were moving. The mag boots worked great for walking at a normal pace, but the fastest way to move given the low ceiling of the corridor was to kick off hard and catch themselves with one hand against the ceiling and push back off, like a ball bouncing off everything.

Zo let Vincent take the lead. He had the most combat experience, and, unlike Grant, he was not careless, and prone to solving everything with explosives. Then Grant, with a hand seemingly always on one of his grenades. Zo followed closely behind, followed by Clarice, Mons, and Rob. She told Jonas to cover their back. He was by far the most skilled at maneuvering in low-g and was the only one moving with anything resembling grace.

***

The XO was screaming over the radio to the security teams in the docking ring.

"Shit. Sir, several breaching pods detected."

"We've identified two destroyer class attackers. No identifiers."

"Brace. Brace! A full rocket barrage incoming. Brace!"

The station shook again. This time the suspension was not enough to prevent the spire itself from shaking.

***

Zo stumbled as the station shook violently. She looked around.

Everyone had grabbed whatever was nearest. Mons was clinging to a door frame. They were all frozen at least five seconds after the shaking stopped, still not sure if it was over.

"What the hell is going on?" Grant exclaimed loudly. He didn't get an answer.

An announcement came over the PA system alerting everyone to stay in their cabins due to an attack, telling all security to report to their station.

Everyone looked at each other.

"Who would be stupid enough to attack Vanguard? I mean, apart from us?"

Vincent grinned at his attempt at a joke, but nobody laughed. Most likely they were *all* wondering who would attack Vanguard.

Zo could only imagine the destruction where the last barrage had hit the station. It couldn't take many barrages like that before the damage would be severe enough for the station to start venting atmosphere.

This wasn't what they'd planned, but hopefully, the confusion would be sufficient to still let them get to the vault.

"Prepare, a group is coming our way."

Vincent had just given the warning and thrown himself behind a cabinet when two guards entered and started firing at them. More were coming, judging by the sounds.

They were being shot at by four or five security officers. Grant lobbed another smoke grenade. They heard coughing through the smoke. Vincent snuck up to the closest guard and stunned him at close range.

Three stumbled backward, around a corner, to try to get away from the smoke.

Only one was left standing, and as soon as Rob saw an outline, he shot at him.

Zo and Vincent started firing at the three who fell back.

"The vault is this way."

With the security team falling back, Grant took the lead and bounced down the corridor in the opposite direction of where the guards had retreated to.

***

"Our fighters are finally launching."

"Sir, Vanguard II reports they have dispatched two fighter wings and are readying four destroyers."

"They've taken out two of our fighters already."

"Sir, Red Wing is reporting the attacking ship appears to have a Mars Colonial insignia."

"Destroyer *Damocles* has launched from Vanguard II. They're not even fully out of port yet and they're already firing."

"Shit . . . Sir! Sir!"

The XO turned toward him.

"Vanguard II is heating up mass drivers, sir."

"Are they lunatics? Tell them to not even think about it. If they fire those things, this whole station will be ripped to shreds."

"Sir, Vanguard II C&C is informing us that given the firepower employed and the Mars insignia, they are treating this as a possible act of war, and they consider us expendable if the attackers can't be taken down otherwise. They apologize and inform us mass driver barrage will be the last resort . . ."

"So they *are* lunatics." The XO looked exasperated.

"Can they do that?"

"I want someone on the line with Earth Military Command NOW. Get someone anywhere up the chain of command to rein in those bastards."

"And order evacuation prep."

The XO was pacing and swearing to himself.

"Destroyer *Luna* is engaging a second attacking vessel."

Chapter 14

They slipped into the room where access to the vault was. It was a fairly standard office.

Grant's first instinct was to try to find something heavy and barricade the door, before they realized it wouldn't help much given the low gravity unless they had someone to secure it against.

Zo and Vincent looked like they knew exactly what to do, however, as they overturned desks for the team to hide behind and pulled out rolls of carbon filaments to tie across the opening—sharp enough and tough enough to prevent anyone from trying to tear through it with their hands.

It wouldn't stop anyone for long by itself, but it'd prevent anyone from running straight into the room, and they'd be exposed while trying to cut it down. Hopefully, it would buy them some time.

Grant left them to it and went into the opening to the vault where he huddled over his equipment to prep the explosive charge.

It wasn't much of a vault, really. More of a secure storage room. The heavy-duty vaults were in the storage decks below. Nobody expected an attack on the spire to steal anything, and the vault here was mostly for administrative needs. It was clear that Vanguard C&C had no idea that anyone valued the canister they were coming for.

A relatively small shaped charge should be enough to force the door, and Grant could have placed his blindfolded.

The explosion was small and just as contained as intended. Grant was pleased with himself and grinned for nobody in particular.

"There! Hear that? They're going for the vault."

They could hear the first security team yelling outside.

***

"Sir, as best we can tell, groups from three breaching pods are now fighting their way towards C&C from three different locations. The last group appears to have just blown the vault. We're not aware of anything valuable held in

74

the vault at present, so the tactical team is unsure what they're looking for."

"Tell security to focus on lockdown at the spire endpoints, and C&C. Let's isolate the group here, and then take them down."

"We have two confirmed breach locations. One in sector G5, the other in section A3. Dispatching security teams."

"Working to pinpoint the last breach position."

"Gamma team is not responding. Echo is searching for the group that breached the vault."

The XO motioned for one of the security team to join Echo team, while the other team remaining in C&C took up posts by the doors.

***

They hurriedly looked through the items in the vault. The container was easy to locate. It was just sitting on a shelf by itself, neatly labeled. Jonas grabbed it and put it in his backpack.

They'd originally intended to go back down the way they came, but now that they were pinned down by security outside, that didn't seem like a viable alternative, and they needed to figure out another option.

Grant could hear the security team outside trying to figure out how to get at them—they'd clearly noticed the filaments.

"Grenade!" Vincent's voice boomed.

It was just a smoke grenade and everyone still had their masks on. Grant could hear plasma fire but could not tell if anyone was getting hit or where exactly it was coming from.

"Grant! Place charges on the outer wall."

It was Jonas, right beside him, though Grant could just barely see his outline through the smoke. Jonas grabbed his wrist and pulled it out in the direction he meant.

Grant caught the drift—they could rappel down, or use the mag-grips to move around the outside to at least get away from the current attackers. Either way, they needed to blow open the outer wall.

The smoke was dissipating. Two security guards were lying unconscious by the door . . . Zo was grabbing at her shoulder, but he couldn't see any

75

blood and she was moving around. The others were hiding behind the overturned tables.

Some of the filament had been cut. It was likely the security team outside might try again, but their two shot team members might make them hesitate for just long enough.

Grant started preparing a second shaped charge on the vault wall/floor.

Thankfully whatever the hell is going on with the attack is keeping most of security busy elsewhere, Grant thought—had they had more people there, they'd likely push ahead much faster.

The security forces just seemed to be waiting, expecting them to have nowhere to go. That'd probably change the moment they heard another explosion. They'd be forced to consider other options, and it wouldn't take the security team long to realize the explosions meant they were heading out.

Zo fired out the doorway again, as it seemed there was some motion out there, and Vincent threw another flashbang as soon as Grant motioned that he was setting off the charge.

Everyone braced. It was precision work—leaving just the right size hole. Jonas quickly started placing mag-grips to hold several ropes in place. Jonas told the rest to hold back a few minutes and then follow.

They heard yelling in the corridor—clearly, the security team had realized they were up to something.

A large flame blasted through the door. The security team had brought a flame thrower to clear the path and make it hard to try to fire back. Zo and Vincent fired as a distraction before they pulled back into the vault with the rest of the team.

Grant just finished placing the rest of his explosives along what remained of the vault door as a parting surprise, and they started climbing out and follow Jonas.

They set a smaller charge against the barricaded door, as a diversion, and dropped several gas canisters as they set everything off to hide what happened.

As soon as the wall was blown open, they *dropped* two ropes. The gravity near the spire was low enough that the ropes just slowly unfurled.

Jonas started lowering and locking himself in position to prepare the route for the rest of them.

Unfortunately, it was now effectively daytime. When C&C called an emergency, the normal cycle had abruptly stopped and lights turned on. They needed to get away as quickly as possible, before anyone realized they could get security lower down to try to shoot at them. The distance to the ground was too far, but from the spokes, they might make nice targets.

As soon as they could see, Jonas had attached the first sets of mag-grips and moved out of view. The rest followed one by one, over the edge by the ropes that were now hanging mostly as you'd expect a rope to hang; the far end affected by enough gravity to pull them somewhat taut when nobody was jostling them, but as they lowered themselves it felt like a very different experience—each movement amplified much more than in Earth gravity.

They ditched what equipment they did not expect to need again, holding on to a few mag-grips and ropes in case, and their weapons.

Grant finally dropped over the edge, and felt queasy as he looked down, but quickly focused on the grips ahead and followed as fast as he could.

Chapter 15

"What did they do? Shit. Did they blow themselves up?"

The team outside the vault had been thrown back when the remaining explosives against the vault door went off, but none of them were hurt. As soon as they got back on their feet, they peered in, but visibility was still not great.

But they could see the light—Vanguard's emergency mode had automatically switched the station to daytime settings, and the floodlights on the spire lit up the volume outside the gaping hole the attackers had left in the vault wall.

"They've blown the wall. Repeat, they've blown a hole in the vault wall. There is no sign of them—they appear to have exited through the hole."

One of the security officers relayed the information to C&C while another stuck his head out and pulled back just in time to avoid having his head taken off by a plasma blast.

"Sir, they're climbing around the outside of the spire."

They tried looking outside again.

***

"First attacking cruiser is down, sir."

"Both *Damocles* and *Luna* are now firing at the second attacker, and the two last destroyers are almost ready to attack."

"Attacking infiltrators in the vault have escaped and appear to be retreating. The three other breaching teams are still advancing."

"We've lost sight of the retreating team, sir. Team on site reports they're preparing to pursue around the outside of the spire. Our other security assets are all tied up with the groups that are still advancing."

***

Jonas rapidly attached mag-grips around the outer edge. He was perfect for this task, he thought to himself. He wasn't quite an acrobat, but his martial arts training had given him a flexibility and agility that let him move rapidly. Their normal jobs didn't often give him a chance to use his abilities like this.

He was fastening grips for the others to follow around the spire, back toward where they had entered, but also along, toward the spoke.

He skillfully threaded a rope through the mag-grips, tied it, and placed another rope. Didn't want to give their pursuers anything to cut. He repeated this several times, before he could see the grips they'd left behind on their way out.

His main worry was that they couldn't risk going down the outside of the spoke the way they came up—it'd make them too visible and easy for station security to catch by waiting at the bottom now that they were alert.

Once he reached the mag-grips they'd left last time, he connected another rope and started making his way back toward the rest in case they needed help.

Clarice was coming toward him first, with the rest of the team following soon afterward. Vincent last. He kept his eye out for any signs of the security team, but didn't see any.

He fixed another rope and started going forward again.

***

Vincent looked back in time to spot one of the Vanguard security guards sticking his head out of the hole and fired off a round. He missed, and hurried on, hoping to get far enough around the edge they wouldn't be able to see him by the time they tried again. He detached the mag-grips behind him as he moved, so they'd be harder to follow this way. Hopefully, it'd take time to figure out how they were escaping.

He moved methodically and smoothly despite his size, attaching and re-attaching himself to the support ropes as he went.

***

Jonas led the team back toward the spoke as quickly as he could, and when

79

he reached where they'd connected, he added additional grips so they could bunch up closer. Clarice and Zo passed him, with Grant right behind.

"Do you have any more explosives?"

Grant shook his head.

"Damn. We really can't risk descending on the outside. It's fine up here, but they can just surround the spoke at the floor level."

Jonas scanned the path ahead of them. There were maintenance hatches on the spoke. They'd not taken them on the way up because the risk of tripping security was too high. But between them, they and the other attackers had already alerted security, and also spread the security forces out.

He swiftly, and somewhat carelessly, swung and attached grips to get himself to the front of the group again.

"Maintenance hatch."

He pointed at the nearest one and moved toward it. It was easy to get open. He climbed in. The others waited.

It was dark inside, and Jonas had to wait a few seconds for his eyes to adjust. Only the emergency lights were on. Nobody there. Jonas stuck his head out and gave a thumbs up. Once they were all inside, Jonas put the grate back on and motioned for everyone to stand back. He fused the grate in place with a plasma pistol; the only one he'd brought. If anyone followed them this way, it'd hopefully slow them down.

Jonas moved over to Zo who was studying the schematics. There was a lift in the spoke, but it'd be a massive risk even if it was still running. There was a staircase leading down from where they were, but it'd hit security doors in three places. The other alternative was back into the spire and working their way past nearly two kilometers of hallways and rooms that likely had some security still in them.

They agreed to take the lift shaft; they had the climbing gear, after all. It meant going back into the spire and dealing with whatever security was guarding the spoke entry points.

Jonas took the lead as they crawled up the maintenance tunnel toward the hub. He peered out and counted at least five members of the security team. They had clearly been to the armory and brought out the heavy weaponry.

Two more guards entered, and Jonas heard them talk.

"C&C reports the people who attacked the vault are unaccounted for but might try to make it in here. They were apparently escaping around the outside of the spire."

"Who are these people?"

Most likely these guards had never needed to deal with anything more than the occasional theft and assorted minor drunken fights. They looked nervous.

Jonas looked back at the team and outlined the guards' positions. They had a problem. They would not be able to make it out of the tunnel very quickly. They might be easy to pin down, and if they threw a smoke grenade, odds were one or the other of the security guards would see where it came from and start firing.

They could wait, but chances of the guards leaving would be low.

He contemplated trying to find one of the junctions in the tunnels and get them into position in two tunnels at once, but there was the risk of making too much noise and getting attacked while in the tunnels. Maybe the staircases would've been better after all.

They were out of flashbangs, so they couldn't stun them either.

"Jonas . . . Jonas . . ."

It was Grant whispering.

"What if you throw a gun into the room with the smoke grenade?"

"It's risky, but if you throw the grenade and then jam the trigger on one of the stun guns and throw it in too, hopefully they won't know where to fire—the sparks will go everywhere."

It was typical of Grant to think up a solution that involved a light-show when he didn't have more explosives. Jonas got out his knife and cut off a piece of rope and got the stun gun ready so he could tie the trigger in place. He nearly set it off, but soon he was ready.

"Ready. As soon as I jump, jump and dive. Make sure you know who you're firing on. Pass it on."

Jonas pried the grate open and threw the smoke grenade. As he expected, he was spotted and soon the tunnel was heating up from the shots from a heavy-duty plasma rifle. He pulled back before aiming his stun gun at the opening and lodging the trigger in place.

81

It was hard to throw properly with such little space, but he jettisoned the gun out far enough that it drew fire from at least three of the guards. He quickly and quietly pulled himself up to the opening, burning his hands on the metal heated by the plasma rounds.

He jumped out, and rolled in a different direction to the gun and ended up rolling on top of one very bewildered guard. Jonas punched him in the face before he could react.

He looked back and saw shadows landing through the smoke.

One of the guards must have realized his gun was a decoy and had disabled it. Three people were firing toward the shadows.

Jonas crept toward one of them and got him in a neck lock, squeezing until the man fell unconscious. The smoke started dissipating, and Jonas made for the second plasma rifle still firing. Someone grabbed his shoulder, and Jonas spun around and almost broke Clarice's neck.

Someone knocked out the last guard standing.

"Quick. I'm sure more will be coming at any moment."

Vincent was already prying one of the lifts open. As soon as he got it open, he motioned for Jonas.

"Start descending. I'm going to open a second one as a decoy."

Jonas started sending the rest rappelling down the shaft. Showing them how to hold on to a pair of mag-grips they could use to slow down or stop if they started moving too fast. Zo went first, followed by Mons and Marcus. Then Grant and Rob.

"Hold on, you go, I have these, remember—I can buy us a bit of extra cover."

Clarice flashed her eyes in red. Vincent had opened the other lift-shaft just as Jonas went.

As he started dropping, Jonas heard several methodical shots.

Chapter 16

As Jonas jumped, Clarice quickly asked Vincent to take out the lights in the tunnels. He blasted off a handful of shots in quick succession to kill the lights in the short open section of the spire in both directions.

He nodded to her, and she thought she could make out an expression of respect for her in covering their escape, on a face she'd always found impossibly hard to read. Maybe she was making it up. He couldn't see her in the darkness with the smoke enveloping her, but her augmented eyes saw him clearly enough.

He quickly followed Jonas down the shaft.

Clarice threw the last smoke grenades down the spire in either direction, and a couple more in the hub.

She turned down the visible light from her eyes and lay quietly.

She could hear voices. Her hearing was augmented too, but nothing as advanced as her eyes. Just one ear, and it was not that much more sensitive. She couldn't tell for sure how close they were. It surprised her they were taking so long—clearly the other attackers were occupying a lot of the security forces, or they'd not yet realized that they'd made it back inside.

Just as she was thinking that, a lone guard was coming down one of the tunnels with a mask on. Clearly some of the people they'd attacked managed to report back about the smoke grenades. Figures.

Clarice lay still next to one of the stunned guards. She knew they weren't dead, but they looked dead. She'd seen dead bodies before on missions, but it was still weird lying up close to motionless bodies spread out in the aftermath of a battle like this. She knew Zo would blame herself if they killed anyone on this mission. It was bad enough they'd had to knock out so many innocent guards. But they had no choice.

The soldier was moving cautiously and getting close. The other voices were getting louder. She got ready to jump him when he clearly noticed her move and she was hit in the shoulder and knocked back.

The pain seared through her as the plasma burned her skin clear off and started tearing through part of her shoulder muscle.

83

While she was paralyzed by pain, her attacker grabbed her and tried to get her in a neck lock. Clarice composed herself quicker than she thought possible as the pain was still filling all of her senses, and she kneed him in the groin.

He wasn't big, but bigger than her, and though he winced in pain, he was still on top of her and having him there triggered a primal fear in her. He punched her face before grabbing her throat with one arm and her right arm with the other. She tried throwing him off her, but it felt like she had no power whatsoever to lift her right arm due to the way the plasma burn had torn her shoulder.

The smoke was starting to clear, and her eyes gave her an even clearer view. He grinned as he tore her mask off and pointed his helmet light straight in her face.

She realized it was probably clear enough from this distance that he must be relaying her face, and if he wasn't, cameras in this room probably caught her . . . They'd have her identity soon enough.

"C&C, come in, I've captured one of the attackers in spoke hub alpha. Several men down here, please send reinforcements."

While he was speaking, she quietly moved her left arm sufficiently close to her side to pull her knife from her thigh holster, and before he realized what was happening, she lifted it and pushed it into his abdomen. He reflexively let go of her to grab at his wound, and she used the opening to get hold of her stun gun and knocked him out with it.

She pushed his bleeding, limp body off her, and propped herself up on her left arm, and crawled to the lift shaft.

After worrying about stunning and beating up guards, she'd stabbed one . . . She felt sick. She hoped he'd make it.

Clarice almost fell headfirst into the lift shaft as she grabbed on with her left hand and started sliding down after the others with her right harm hanging disabled by her side.

***

"All breaching teams are now retreating, sir. Appears the remaining attacking cruiser is heating their engines. Looks like they're giving up."

"Security in pursuit of the invading forces. Spire security reports they've done a sweep and no sign of remaining intruders in the central section. Lockdown appears to be secure."

"They appear to have gone down one of the lift shafts, and gotten out on one of the habitation levels. We're checking cameras, but so far the only face we have is the one we got from spoke hub alpha, where they escaped."

It seemed like it was over almost as soon as it started. The second attacking cruiser was firing engines and appeared to be limping out into nowhere. The C&C staff looked for possible routes that made sense, but could find nothing.

As far as they could tell, two of the breaching crews were able to make it back before they split.

The third was blown out of the sky as the cruiser Ulysses hit their pod on the way back. The fourth crew wasn't found, but a station sweep found nothing and it was presumed they were in one of the escaped breaching pods.

"Brace!"

They'd relaxed too soon. As the escaping cruiser was accelerating at hazardous rates away on a trajectory whose only benefit seemed to be to put the moon between it and Vanguard II, it launched its remaining rockets on a wide spread along Vanguard.

"We're leaking atmosphere."

The Vanguard XO wiped blood from his face from a minor cut and ordered a full evacuation.

Chapter 17

Zo looked around the corner and motioned for everyone to follow her. They'd all gotten down okay, seemingly without being spotted. Getting out of the spoke lift shaft proved easy enough—the evacuation alarm sounded as they were looking to see what they were dealing with, and the guards ran to help guide people out.

Clarice had been last out, and Zo gasped when she saw her limp arm and her bruises. She rushed over to check how Clarice was doing. Rob was putting a numbing agent on her shoulder and dressing it.

"It'll be okay. It'll scar and will take some time to heal, but it should be okay."

Zo trusted Rob's judgment and, as much as she wanted to make sure Clarice was alright, she needed to take stock of everyone. She brushed Clarice's left shoulder gently and gave her a smile, then nodded toward the others.

"This is Vanguard Command. Please proceed to the docking area as quickly as possible. The station is venting atmosphere. This is an evacuation."

The notice boomed over the loudspeakers, then repeated.

They all removed their gas masks and harnesses and threw them in a corner. They did not have time to change, but put on their flight jackets over the outfits they'd worn, and hoped nobody would notice as they hurried toward the exits. The paths were filling with people hurrying out in various levels of dress and undress. They decided to spread out. Zo took Clarice's arm and supported her.

They were close to the docking area when they saw guards.

"The guard in the hub put a light in my face. They might have my picture . . ."

She paused.

" . . . and . . . and I might have killed him. I stabbed him in the abdomen," Clarice whispered in Zo's ear and looked down.

In the rush, they were the first words she'd spoken since she got down. Zo grabbed a bandana from her bag and tied it so Clarice's hair was purposefully covering more of her face.

"Keep looking down. And change your eye color. It will be okay."

Clarice thought for a second about what her eyes had looked like when she was spotted, and her eyes briefly sparkled before settling on a steely blue.

They walked at a brisk pace toward the guards. Zo intentionally walked as close as possible to one of them, almost pushing up against him, and looked him straight in the eyes.

"Excuse us, please."

"Is your friend okay?"

The guard looked at Clarice's arm that hung limp with a look of genuine concern.

"She fell and hurt her arm. She'll be fine, we have a ship medic; he'll take care of it once we're out."

The guard nodded and called a colleague over.

"Escort these two to their ship; she's got an injury."

"Thank you so much." Zo's gratitude was genuine and she even smiled at the guard.

A scared-looking junior guard who'd probably never dealt with a situation like this before shielded Clarice's right side and walked them to the security control where there was total chaos as everyone was being scanned and accounted for.

Zo was looking around with a worried look as their escort asked them to hold on for a moment and walked over to one of the checkpoints.

Zo tightened her grip around a small stun gun in her pocket as the guard came back with one of the people manning the checkpoints.

"My friend here will take care of you. Good luck."

They thanked their escort and followed the checkpoint guard who motioned them over to a closed lane and just waved them through.

Just as they were about to walk away, he called for them. Zo clutched the gun.

"Sorry, just need to take down your ship's name."

Zo told him, and he wrote it down on his pad and thanked them.

87

They hurried to the nearest lift, squeezed in, and were taken to the right docking level.

When they got to their ship, everyone else was already there. Zo finally exhaled fully and took a few deep breaths to calm her nerves.

It took a few minutes to get their clearance to leave and another couple of minutes to accelerate out of the station.

***

They sped toward the Moon-Mars gate which was half an hour away at the highest acceleration Rob was prepared to agree to given Clarice's injury.

"We have a problem."

Jonas had taken Clarice's station and was working the comms.

"Apparently they're restricting access to the Mars gate. No indication why, but I assume it has to do with Vanguard. Maybe they think the attackers are Mars separatists."

"Head for the belt gate then."

There were multiple belt gates, as the asteroids of interest in the belt had a wide range of orbital periods and so gates were needed for different areas, but there was only one gate to the belt near the Moon.

The Moon-belt gate exited near Ceres, the largest asteroid in the asteroid belt by a large factor. Ceres was also orbited by gates to Earth, Mars, as well as two other parts of the belt, so it would give them options.

***

The detour wouldn't be particularly long, and hopefully, the belt-Mars gates would remain open. If not, they'd have to find somewhere suitable to wait it out there. Much safer than near-Earth space, certainly.

Jonas adjusted course and continued following instructions. Clarice had given him access to one of her programs that would alter their idents. They'd used them before, on smuggling runs. Usually these things were not checked that thoroughly, because nobody was that interested, but even if they were,

88

Morgan had ensured any discrepancies would plausibly look like a result of damage.

Outside, the *Black Rain* looked like a fairly common freight ship. They'd named her after her shape—an oblong, dark shape, almost like a drop, occasionally glinting where light hit her. It was painted darker than most, making it harder to spot with your bare eyes, but not dark enough to be unusual. More importantly, the paint they'd applied absorbed and scattered radar enough to make them harder to spot on scans. It by no means made them invisible—doing so would itself have set off all kinds of red flags, but it gave them a minor advantage at a distance, and every little bit helped.

Especially if they had to hide somewhere like the belt.

They arrived at the Moon-belt gate without incident.

The gates themselves were without security. They were designed to transport anything that moved within their source volume to their destination volume no matter what. The Centauri design just worked that way, and no attempt to reverse engineer their tech had so far revealed how to reprogram the things to add an authentication or authorization mechanism.

But the Earth cruiser sitting near the gate waiting for an excuse to fire was another matter. They demanded idents from passing ships and reserved the right to intervene. Normally, it was a quick automated check and nothing else.

The ident *Jolly Roger* was accepted without question, but Jonas made a note to suggest to Clarice that perhaps she should pick slightly less on-the-nose names for fake idents they used primarily when evading the law.

When through, they queried a nearby private station about the status of travel to Mars.

"This is Jolly Roger to station. We're wondering if you could update us on the status of travel onwards to Mars."

"Welcome to the neighborhood. This is *Jones' Folly* C&C. "

A brief period of static followed.

"Jolly Roger, *huh*? Bet they love that in near-Earth space. Got it painted on your hull too?"

"No, just the name. More trouble than it's worth, really. Thinking of changing it again. Can you help us with updates on the Mars gate or not?"

"Yeah, yeah, Jolly Roger. *Arr.*"

Their message was followed by laughter. Jonas didn't share their sense of humor.

"Ok, okay, sorry. We don't get much entertainment out here. Or traffic. Last update is that the Ceres-Mars gate is still open, but to expect additional screening, whatever the hell that will mean."

"This whole thing is bound to be bad for business."

The station operator was chatty and eager to hear about what had happened at Vanguard. In return for some scraps of details from Jonas that hadn't been broadcast, they got a friendly admonition to be careful. For the "additional screening" presumably.

An Earth destroyer was lurking near the Ceres-Mars gate—Earth was even less popular in the belt than near Mars, and an Earth destroyer even more so. Having a destroyer lurking around would undoubtedly be bad for business, as the operator had said.

They flew past the station at a good distance, far enough that when Jonas changed course, it put them on a course that made it plausible to claim to anyone nosy enough to ask that they were returning from a freight run. Jonas lowered the acceleration—it'd add a couple of hours, but he hoped it'd make them look like a freighter more concerned about fuel cost than how soon they'd get there.

They got a final, "*Arr!*" over comms from the station operator and more laughter as they were leaving.

Jonas cycled the fake ident again. They'd be the *Black Pearl* this time, and Jonas was slightly amused: not enough to laugh—but more annoyed.

Chapter 18

As soon as they were certain they weren't being followed, the atmosphere relaxed, and everyone spread out to check on the ship. They were going to be coasting towards the nearest belt-Mars gate for a while, making it easier to move about the ship thanks to zero gravity.

Vincent had taken over for Jonas on the bridge and was helping Zo to verify that all systems were okay. As soon as they were satisfied, their attention turned to the box they'd stolen.

Something felt off. The attack couldn't have been a coincidence. The level of fire-power involved was crazy. As far as Captain Ortega knew, it was the first time anyone had caused a full evacuation due to venting atmosphere on any major station.

"So, what's in this damn thing?"

Vincent's voice was quiet and deep, and he looked at Zo with the kind of concerned look she had only seen on him when trying to determine whether to shoot at something or hide—a mix of concern and anger triggered, in this case, by the far too coincidental large scale attack on Vanguard.

"They said it was evidence of plans for invasion by the Centauri. With physical evidence to prove that is where it's from."

"You've told us what they said. But if someone else powerful enough to risk an attack on Vanguard also wants it? Who the hell knows if they told the truth?"

"Yeah, I'm having concerns too, Vincent."

Zo handled the container carefully. It looked like a fairly standard nondescript lockbox. Nothing fancy. Not even a fingerprint scanner, but a code and a key. No sign of any attempt to force it open. Vanguard security clearly didn't think the contents were any of their business—just held on to it until someone got around to dealing with the courier.

More worrying was the fact that, clearly, someone knew there was something important on Vanguard. Nobody would attempt a crazy full-on attack like that if they didn't hope for a massive payoff, would they?

"Let's open it."

Vincent was motioning for Zo to hand over the box, but she made no move to give it to him.

"Maybe. But let's use the medi-scanner first and see what we can learn. If we ruin whatever physical evidence is in the box, and it is what they said it was, we'll have really fucked up."

Vincent grumbled a little, but shrugged his shoulders and cracked a narrow smile. He might be impatient, but Zo knew he was the ultimate pragmatist on the team, always patient when he knew patience would likely get him his way without wasting effort on arguing.

He led the way toward sickbay, where Rob was finishing up checks on Clarice's shoulder. She'd regained some motion in her arm and was deep in a discussion with Rob about whether to augment it. Zo pursed her lips—she was not a fan of augmentation, and wished Clarice wasn't so enthusiastic about it, but she turned towards her and gave her a smile.

"How is the arm?"

"Been better," Clarice said through a pained grin.

"Why have you brought the box?"

"Vincent wants to break it open. I want to scan it before we decide."

She handed it to Rob.

"See what you can do with it, please. Nothing too high power, remember there's a storage device in there."

Rob placed the box in their scanner and adjusted the settings to account for a metal box rather than a squishy human. They all looked at the screen. The first scan yielded nothing—the box was unusually well shielded. Maybe just on account of the storage unit.

Rob tried increasing the intensity. They could see an outline of a storage stick, and an entirely opaque mass that seemed like it might be cylindrical.

"If that's a storage device, I can't increase settings further without taking the risk of damaging it. If you want to know what that other box is, I'm afraid you'll need to open it up."

"Thanks, Rob."

Zo was still not sure they should open the box, but Vincent looked at her with a face that made it very clear what he thought.

"Okay. Let's go to the workshop, Vincent," Zo finally said.

Clarice tagged along.

Their workshop was well equipped, but looked very much unlike Earth-style workshops. Zo hadn't spent much time here. She wasn't someone who had much interest in hardware other than using it.

The whole room had a lock. No full-on airlock procedure to enter and exit, but as needed, on exit, they'd get a quick and effective vacuum. The door could be fully sealed. Avoiding the spread of material that might be unhealthy to breathe was a major consideration for any spaceship design.

Zero, or *just* low-g, created a lot of other constraints. The risk of sudden changes in acceleration, not just up and down, but directional, created additional issues. Things that could be reasonably expected to stay in one place in a stationary workshop could float around for ages, or suddenly become missiles.

Every smallest tool was locked into place and the workstations had covers and special mounts to prevent most of the dust or particles created from working on materials from spreading out, and the vacuum lock to minimize what got out.

It was a small room. Uncomfortably so during acceleration when they had to pick a floor. Better when coasting, like now when they could use every wall.

They didn't have any reason to expect any particles, so they didn't bother putting the box into any of the covered workstations. Vincent got out some tools and tried removing the lock panel first. It proved more resistant than he expected, but suddenly it came loose.

"Shit."

"What's wrong?" Zo leaned over to look.

"Hear that sound? I think we tripped something."

Zo could hear a faint noise from inside the box.

"What do you mean, something? A bomb? Self-destruct?"

"What the hell do I know? I didn't build this damn thing but we need to find out fast."

Vincent picked up the pace and managed to disable the lock and open the box. The box was not built to be particularly hard to open. When he opened it up, he found out why.

The *box* inside they were not able to penetrate with their scanning equipment appeared to be a gas cylinder. The sound they'd heard was a leak.

Vincent started coughing.

"Out! Now!" He gasped.

They all bolted for the door. Vincent stumbled and went down on his knees. Zo and Clarice had to pull him into the lock.

"Override the damn vacuum procedure," Zo yelled.

Clarice entered the codes as quickly as she could and the outer door opened. Zo was coughing, her sight blurring.

"Hurry. Seal the door after us . . ." Her voice was fading. Clarice got the door open, and together they managed to drag Vincent, now unconscious, out of the lock and seal the door, just as Zo felt herself fade out of consciousness too.

***

"How are you feeling?"

Rob was standing over Zo in sickbay. She couldn't recall what had happened at first, tried to get up, and almost lost consciousness again.

"Easy. You breathed in quite a lot of whatever the hell that gas was."

Zo opened her mouth to speak.

"Before you ask, I'm still analyzing it. It looks like a sedative. Not meant to kill, but there are always risks at high concentrations anyway."

Zo looked around, and saw Vincent still unconscious and hooked up to a breathing mask.

"He's still alive, but he breathed in a lot more than you. We won't know for a while if there's any damage."

"Clarice?"

Zo's voice was weak and raspy.

"She's fine. She hit the alarm and then got the workshop fully sealed and purged as soon as we'd gotten Vincent and you here."

The dizziness was slowly dissipating, and Zo managed to move up a tiny bit before the exertion made it worse again. She drifted in and out of consciousness for a bit.

"Cap?"

She opened her eyes, not sure how much time had passed. Clarice was standing over her.

"We cycled the air in the workshop and were able to have a closer look. The only thing in there is a data storage unit, and all the data on it is encrypted. Damn pointless exercise."

This was the closest to rage Zo had ever seen from Clarice. Her face was hard and angry, her fists clenched. She was never the particularly emotional type. As long as Zo had known her, she'd always been guarded, even in private.

"You didn't touch it did you?" Zo was worried they'd have ruined any fingerprints or DNA evidence.

"Don't worry, we were careful. Used one of the surgical robot arms to pick it up and insert it."

Of course she did, was Zo's last thought before once again drifting out of consciousness.

When Zo woke up again, she felt much better. Clarice was gone, but Rob was there. She'd slept for eight hours. Vincent was better, according to Rob. He'd briefly regained consciousness and seemed coherent for a few minutes before going out like a light again.

"He'll be okay, probably. He's strong. Judging by how much longer it took him to wake up than you, he'll probably be out of commission for another day."

"Thanks, Doc. I need to get to the bridge."

"You're too weak. Rest some more first, please."

"Can't. I'll take it easy; I promise."

Zo got up slowly. She was a bit unsteady, but pushed Rob's hand away when he tried to help.

"At least let me have someone go with you, in case you pass out."

Zo nodded, and Rob called Mons. Mons looked slightly annoyed at babysitting duty, but dutifully followed Zo to the bridge. When there, he took his station.

"Status, please," was all Zo said as she sunk down into her seat, more exhausted than she wanted to let on from the short trip.

95

Jonas turned towards her.

"Glad to see you're okay, Cap. We're within an hour of the Ceres-Mars gate. We slowed down when you went out of commission—didn't want to risk being subjected to a search and have to explain."

"No communication from the Earth destroyer, though it has to have noticed us several hours ago."

Clarice bounced over to her. "Captain, there's something else you should know about the box. I didn't get to tell you before you passed out again. After we copied the contents, we put it back in the scanner, and did some non-invasive scans for DNA or any other organic matter."

Clarice paused.

"And?"

"There was none. Not a hint. Whoever handled this thing was extremely careful and used gloves *and* wiped it down. Whatever physical evidence Sovereign Earth expects there to be on this, there's nothing. Either their agent didn't check, or messed up, or they didn't tell us the truth."

Zo didn't know how to react and was quiet for a bit.

"Well, we'll just have to see what they say when we drop it off, won't we."

Chapter 19

The Earth destroyer lay motionless nearby, but didn't even hail them, whether thanks to Clarice's fake ident or they were just not considered interesting enough.

And so, they obtained passage through the Ceres-Mars gate without incident. At least one good sign.

They arrived in Mars orbit near Phobos, Mars' larger moon and also its innermost moon. Security was much tighter than usual—the gate flanked by two Mars colonial destroyers with a contingent of smaller ships showing up on their scanners. The Vanguard attack appeared to have left the government seriously spooked.

The newsfeed told them military ships were being deployed across the entire Sol gate network.

Shortly afterward, Mars gate control located on one of the colonial destroyers informed them of additional extraordinary security measures related to the Vanguard attack.

"Report to Hercules Station security for secondary screening. Access to further space is only allowed after being screened. Failure to comply will lead to use of force."

"Understood, Gate Control."

Vincent grimaced. "Yikes. They've not been this on edge since the attempted insurrection in '25."

"You're really showing your age, Grandpa." Clarice smiled and winked at him before adjusting their heading toward Hercules.

Hercules Station was named after the Roman equivalent to the Greek Herakles—a warrior and worshipper of Phobos, who gave name to the Martian moon with the closest orbit.

Hercules was the main military station around Mars, occupying the same orbit as Phobos, offset about halfway between Phobos and the Mars-Earth gate also in the same orbit. The station also hosted off-world cargo processing for ships partitioning cargo for Mars, the moons, and the more than a dozen stations in Mars' orbit.

The Mars-belt gates were somewhat further out, so it would take them some time to match speed. Thankfully, the orbital periods for both were short enough that, though they shifted in relation to each other, it wouldn't take more than a couple of hours to get in a holding pattern near Hercules.

Officially, the station was Mars controlled, but it had a significant Earth military presence. According to the Mars government, because they had been *invited*, while Earth insisted it was their sovereign right.

Chatter on the local net soon confirmed the tension between the two was higher than ever. Rumors had it that the Vanguard attackers had ships with Mars Colonial insignia, and conspiracy theories abounded, claiming it was a false flag operation by Earth to justify a clampdown, while others claimed it was separatists. Some suggested it was aliens.

They approached to within the requested distance from Hercules Station, noted weapons locks with several weapons-stations hot and ready while they were far outside their own weapons-range. Seemed the incident had made everyone trigger happy. They submitted the requested identifying information.

"Wonder if they'll want to inspect the ship," Jonas said.

Zo looked up. "I can't imagine. They don't have the manpower. Anything heading down to Mars will be inspected there anyway."

The clearance didn't take long and they didn't request an inspection.

They began another orbital transfer. This time out toward Deimos' orbit—Mars's second moon. They were very happy to get out of the targets of Hercules Station.

Their target was Nautilus. A small, private station in an orbit not much further in than Deimos'. They adjusted their speed carefully so they would intersect the orbit near the station. They were lucky with their timing—Nautilus was currently in a position allowing them to make the transfer in just a few hours.

Mars space had been getting crowded since the colony exploded in growth. The Moon didn't see quite the same thing due to the proximity of Earth—those wishing to cover Luna Colony often just did so from Earth orbit.

Those wanting to be further from Earth influence, on the other hand, had little to gain from being as close as the Moon: the Moon itself was within the range of the huge mass drivers set up as part of the Earth defense network, and Earth destroyers were spread out so they were never more than an hour away from the combined Earth-Moon space by direct flight, less near major stations and the gates.

Mars was just close enough, yet with the growing colony, also civilized enough to be attractive, yet far enough not to feel overwhelmed by the projection of power of Earth. Somewhat helped by the Mars Colony government, which, though indirectly under the control of Earth through the Earth-dominated United Sol Congress and President, did their utmost to exercise what control they could over local space to the continuous frustration of Earth.

As a result, dozens of private stations were dotted around Mars' space, interspersed between the moons. They ranged from staging stations for large industrial complexes with mining operations in the belt, via rich people's playgrounds, to political and spiritual movements that for one reason or another felt uncomfortable being within closer reach of planet-bound governments.

The stations also included a small number of larger military stations, including the *Mars native* Deimos Guardian (Sovereign Earth supporters angrily pointed out that *Deimos* in Greek mythology is the personification of terror—the Mars government had built a station effectively called Terror Guardian, and expected Earth to think they had only peaceful intentions?) that was built largely as a symbolic outer perimeter defense of sorts, and the Earth-provided Hercules Station, as well as two government-sponsored commercial open trading stations.

The belt had more stations overall, but spread out over a long section of the asteroid belt orbit. The romantic notion of the belt was rocks flying everywhere, but the density is low enough that in most places you will not see anything in any direction, and the stations did little to change that.

Most belt stations were also fairly small compared to the size of the bigger Mars stations, but none were yet anywhere near the size of Vanguard or Vanguard II.

Mars was the only place in the system outside of Earth-Luna space with that many stations in that close a proximity. The Io and Europa colonies were

99

too small to justify more than satellites and a tiny transfer station. There were stations around Jupiter, but mostly scientific. Little trade. Exploration of Neptune and Pluto was underway, but still purely ship-based with no separate local gate control, and so far, little reason to expand trade and commercial stations—too dark and cold and yearlong transfer times to be appealing even for the outlaws.

During the transfer, they looked up what was known about Nautilus, and Clarice *borrowed* some information from a couple of poorly protected private data banks to find out more. What they could dig up was limited.

Nautilus station was owned by one Sebastien Terrell, a rich industrial magnate with extensive trade with mining companies in the belt. Known connections to Sovereign Earth as a donor, but not apparently connected to the leadership other than through money.

The station appeared to have limited trade—it was mostly a playground for Terrell, who had apparently modeled the interior on the descriptions of the fictional Nautilus in Jules Verne's *20,000 Leagues under the Sea*.

They found no blueprints, only a handful of pictures, and the odd blurb here and there about some decadent party full of celebrities that the journalists were noticeably offended they'd failed to get into or get more information about.

Chapter 20

They approached Nautilus slowly while waiting for a confirmation they were welcome to dock. It didn't take long before it came.

The station was twenty years old, but had been extended since. The public drawings implied some defensive weapons, but it was clear from just looking at the exterior of the station that what little they had gleaned from the public data banks was very much outdated. There was no obligation to file plans, and clearly, the owners of Nautilus had not been interested in disclosing much.

They executed a few small extra burns to fully match Nautilus' speed and rotation, then approached slowly towards the docking port.

"Weapons lock, Captain."

Morgan didn't look overly concerned.

"They've not powered up anything. Besides, I guess they want the damn box before shooting us anyway."

There were obvious additional weapons platforms. Obvious not least because they detected weapons locks from places not covered by the original plans.

Zo's concerns had grown steadily since the attack on Vanguard. She'd ruminated on the unknown attackers, then the gas in the storage container put her further on edge. She could not help wondering if there were further surprises in store.

"When we get there, I want us to split up."

"Sovereign Earth doesn't know the size of the crew."

While it'd be conceivable they could have obtained it, it was no harder than suggesting some had been let off.

"Clarice, Grant, and Mons, I want you to stay behind. Hide aboard the ship. While we talk to our contact, you three try to sneak off the ship and see if you can find out if they're telling us the truth."

"Any questions?"

Zo looked from person to person.

"Are you sure this is a good idea, Captain?" Mons asked. "If we're caught, it will look very bad. I mean, we have no evidence they're up to anything."

"You're just scared." Vincent didn't for a moment think Mons' main concern was whether or not the idea was good, but whether or not his skin was on the line.

"I agree with Mons. It's a massive violation of their trust, and who knows what they'll do if they catch us." Grant looked more worried than Mons.

"It's not up for discussion. Between the *coincidence* of the other attack on Vanguard, and the overzealous protective measures of the container we weren't warned about, I want to cover our behinds. Just don't get caught."

Zo was annoyed. She encouraged her crew to speak their mind, and most of the time their decisions were, if not democratic, then at least collaborative. But it was her ship and she was ultimately responsible. If they found nothing, then great. She wanted nothing more than for her fears to be unfounded. But she'd survived this long in the game by being careful.

Once they were lined up with the docking port and close enough, they let the automated systems take over. The docking was routine.

***

A few minutes later, Zo and the rest of the crew were greeted by a number of armed guards in nondescript security uniforms right inside the docking port.

Clarice, Grant, and Mons had left the bridge and were safely hidden in their storage compartments. A benefit of their line of business was that the ship had a number of *unorthodox* well-hidden adjustments to the storage compartments intended for smuggling. They weren't comfortable to hide in, but they would hopefully be more than sufficient to fool any attempt by Nautilus security to search the ship.

"Thank you for joining us. Please come with me."

The man talking was well groomed, with a plump face but otherwise slim build. He was dressed in a suit, rather than a uniform or flight suit. Not what you'd generally expect in a space station docking area.

He motioned to one of the guards.

"You, take two men and check they didn't bring any guests they've failed to tell us about, and then put the ship under guard."

He turned back towards Zo.

"Apologies, Captain, but I'm sure you understand why we want to be cautious."

Zo nodded to him. She did understand.

Looks were exchanged, but Zo wasn't particularly worried and imagined the others weren't either. The extra compartments had remained undetected even when the ship had been subjected to rather extensive searches by both Earth and Mars security in the past.

The key was to hide the extra spaces in areas where noticing unaccounted for volume would require crawling into access tunnels in unpleasant sections and determining that the size of some sections appeared different from the inside vs. outside.

Only the really thorough searches included more than cursory searches—with drones—of the access tunnels in the first place. But when they searched the tunnels, they were looking for goods or people in the tunnels, not access from the tunnels into unaccounted for, undersized rooms or maintenance tunnels that turned this way or that way a bit before they should.

The crew let the guards search them for weapons, and when everybody was satisfied they weren't carrying anything, they followed the man in the suit, with four guards following them.

***

Mons didn't like confined spaces. He had found himself in one, and it annoyed him. He didn't need to be here. It's not like this would make any kind of difference. He was almost doubled over in a compartment that had been created by reducing the size of a water tank by welding a plate part-way in. It was impressively hard to notice the hatch and breathing holes that had been cut into the tank. They were disguised as maintenance panels to replace biofilters, but the filter block swung aside to give just enough space for a

103

grown man to crawl in legs first, bend over, and pull it shut.

Mons had made it clear to Zo he thought the whole thing was pointless, but when she insisted, he wasn't the type to continue arguing, so he bore his resentment quietly.

Soon, he heard the Nautilus security team carrying out their search. It sounded like one of them was right next to the tank he was in. He wasn't particularly nervous, but the sensation of being enclosed on all sides and unable to move unless he released the hatch and so exposed himself was unnerving. He was sweating, and his breath became fast and shallow.

He waited and tried to calm himself down by counting his breaths. He lost count several times and realized he had no idea how many minutes he'd been in there when he heard knocking on the wall in the pattern they'd agreed.

He opened the door, and Clarice and Grant helped him out.

***

"They've left. We'll leave it a bit longer before we try to sneak out. In the meantime, I'll try to do some non-invasive scans of the station."

Clarice bounced toward the bridge. Nautilus spun slowly, and their perceived gravity was only half moon gravity. Their mag boots would easily pull them down from a couple of centimeters and hold them in place, but even a small step could send them flying in a big arc down the corridor.

She looked back. Mons was right behind her, but Grant was walking slowly and cautiously. Grant didn't like low gravity. He was certainly not about to bounce around.

Clarice smiled, entered the bridge, and went to her station. Mons came up to her to look while she started scanning. She couldn't do much without triggering station security. Nothing particularly interesting came up—she could get a decent idea about the overall mass of the station and any big concentrations of mass or open spaces.

Her programs tried to extrapolate something a bit like a map from that, by applying assumptions about different types of equipment and their composition, but it was quite speculative. It'd give them some ideas of which areas to check.

"I think I have an idea to refine the scan further," she told Mons. "I just have to—"

Just then, Grant entered the bridge and at the same moment they heard yelling. Had they been wrong about security leaving the ship? Clarice had checked internal sensors . . . She checked them again—three guards had just re-entered. She looked to Mons and Grant in panic—they couldn't go back to the spaces where they hid last.

Chapter 21

Zo and the rest of her group were led out of the docking area, and through a wide corridor that looked unusual for a space station—it had a kind of steampunk feel to it, with riveted joints and visible plating that would have been dated a century ago.

They were brought to an entrance that looked like the doors to an old stately home that appeared even more out of place. One of the guards keyed in a code and the doors that resembled Earth-style doors that'd swing open, instead pulled to the side.

They were led into what seemed like private living quarters, though far more opulent than anything they'd expect on a space station.

The decor lived up to the station name, with a large open living space with a mezzanine and doorways leading off to other areas, decorated with dark polished oak and ebony furniture, ornate brass hand-rails, a number of clearly fake port-holes (as they, as far as they could tell, were nowhere near the exterior of the station), and a massive chandelier with thousands of crystals, suspended in the middle of the room. The walls were covered with old paintings.

It was quite clear the owner was obsessed with *20,000 Leagues Under the Sea*, and had probably read it more times than any reasonable person would, trying to find ways of adapting the description of the interior of Captain Nemo's infamous submarine to the complexities of a low gravity environment.

"Welcome!"

Another suit-clad man appeared in a doorway at the far end of the room while they were taking it in, and the proclamation boomed out of him accompanied by a grand gesture of the arms that conveyed an expectation of awe on behalf of his newly acquired audience.

"I'm sure you're all terribly worried after that whole affair with Vanguard, but I think you'll be less so after we have a little chat. Or possibly more so, but less worried about your personal safety and more about the world overall."

The man sounded a bit too happy to see them in a way that conveyed more a sense of a salesman than a friend. He also sounded as if he was in the process of welcoming them to a party, if it hadn't been for the contents of the words he had just uttered.

He had a big smile on his face that looked like it had been bought and plastered on—nothing about it looked real, including the whiter than normal teeth.

Zo felt an instinctive distaste for him, but attempted to look pleased to see him.

He motioned them over to a large table in what appeared to be solid oak to one side of the room.

"Please sit."

The first suit-clad man pointed them at the chairs surrounding the large oak table.

"I assume you have the box." He turned toward Zo, who nodded.

"Great. But first, introductions!"

He paused and smiled.

"I am, Sebastien . . . Terrell . . ."

He said his name as if he were expecting applause.

He is probably used to getting it, Zo thought to herself.

"I'm sure you've heard of me. Or if you hadn't, I'm sure you looked up Nautilus and then looked me up."

His fake grin lit up again.

"I'm sure your captain also informed you that Sovereign Earth gave you this job, and that I'm linked through it via donations. As you have probably guessed since I'm the one welcoming you, I'm a bit more involved than that. *Shhh . . .*"

An exaggerated wink did nothing to make him look more genuine.

He asked them to introduce themselves and they went around the table telling him a few words. The whole thing felt surreal. He acted as if they were in an ordinary business meeting in some ordinary boardroom.

"Drinks, please."

He motioned to one of his staff to serve them.

Zo hesitated for a moment, then spoke.

107

"Mr. Terrell, we had some problems with the container. It was damaged."

Terrell's face darkened noticeably.

"The storage device inside is safe, and the physical evidence should be intact. I have it right here," Zo added quickly, and pulled out the storage container wrapped with a sealed hard-plastic casing.

"Since the container was damaged, I had my medic over there," Zo pointed at Rob, "move the storage device into this to preserve any DNA, etc."

Terrell seemed slightly relieved.

"Tell me what happened, please."

Zo recounted the affair with the gas and how they'd removed the storage container after that. But she didn't tell him they'd tried tampering with it when the gas canister was set off. Instead, she insisted it had probably been damaged during their escape from Vanguard.

"I'm so sorry you had to go through that. I had no idea our operative had gone to those lengths."

Terrell did seem genuinely upset about that.

Zo slid the storage device sealed in the new canister over to Terrell. He eagerly grabbed it and immediately plugged the exposed connector into a computer by his seat, spending a minute or so typing.

"It all checks out, Captain Ortega."

Terrell was cheerful again, but it struck Zo the moment he plugged it in he only cared about the storage unit, not the physical evidence their representative had insisted was so critical and the reason they couldn't just transmit the data.

What could he possibly have needed? she thought to herself.

"I cannot thank you enough for your services, Captain Ortega. Your payment will be transferred momentarily."

He nodded to another man who went into a side room.

"Thank you, sir. Though if I may ask you a question, do you have any theory about who the attackers who hit Vanguard were? It's just that it seemed like an awfully weird coincidence. Did they know about the container too?"

"I really know nothing about that, Ortega, it also worries us. But let us not dwell on that! Let me show you around, then join me for dinner."

Zo made some half-hearted attempts at excuses, but didn't push it as it was just what they needed to give Clarice a chance to poke around.

Chapter 22

Grant knew just what to do as they heard the search team get closer. He motioned to Mons and Clarice to follow him and bolted out the bridge exit leading toward the rear of the ship.

On the way, they picked up three spacesuits.

Mons seemed like he was about to ask what they needed the suits for, but Grant held his finger up to his mouth to indicate they still needed to stay quiet. They moved on, bouncing toward the back as quickly as they could.

They could hear the search party behind them—there must be more than three of them by now.

Grant started worrying they might not get around the corner before one of the guards saw or heard them, but they made it past engineering and turned left out of the main corridor in time.

All three entered the recycling plant and Grant closed the door.

"Here. We can hide in the waste water tank."

It held the waste water that had not yet passed through to the final recycling stages.

"Nobody will look there, if they look in this room at all."

"Your plan stinks."

Clarice made her snarky comment completely deadpan, and looked violently unenthusiastic about the idea, but conceded he was right exactly for that reason.

They didn't have time to argue or find somewhere better in any case, and so they all put their suits on quickly.

They were about to slip into the tank when Clarice pointed out she wasn't sure whether or not it could be opened from the inside. She went in first, and closed the tank and tried to open it, and it would not budge. Grant had to open it.

"Shit. Good thing you're here, or Mons and I might have been stuck."

Grant grinned as Clarice stuck just one finger out of the tank. He looked over the locking mechanism. It was simple—it wasn't intended to keep anyone out, after all, just to keep the door in place. He jammed it, and they tested it a few times to make sure.

Mons slipped in next. As he slid in after the others, Grant was happy they couldn't smell the sludge they were dipping into with the suits on. It smelled bad enough earlier before they put them on while the tank was still closed, but they certainly could see everything now, and he wished he didn't have to do that either.

They waited quietly for any indications the search was over and realized they'd have no way of properly telling until they exited the tank. Grant could see Mons was struggling in the confined space, grabbed his shoulders, and made a motion for Mons to focus on his face.

They'd not had time to ensure the suits' comm systems would work without the sound being available to the search party, so he couldn't reassure Mons verbally without being far too loud, but he seemed to be calming down.

After what seemed like an endless wait, someone entered the room and Grant could vaguely hear them moving things around, but nobody opened the waste water container. They rummaged around some more in the corridor outside.

Then there was the occasional clank as they searched further down the corridor or even engineering or the engine room.

After a while the noises stopped, but he couldn't be sure what that meant. Maybe they were still onboard, but just further ahead. They waited what Grant thought was a few minutes more.

Then, he quietly opened the tank lid a little bit and peered out. Nobody was in the room, so he opened it further and climbed out.

When he took off his helmet, Grant almost retched as he smelled what they'd been covered in.

He motioned for the others to remain there while he looked into the hallway outside. There was no sign of anyone, but he waited another two minutes.

When he still couldn't hear anyone, he closed the door and helped Clarice and Mons out.

He could see on the others' faces that they had a similar reaction to his when they took their helmets off. They did their best to get the suits off without getting any of the sludge on their clothes, but they all reeked as they started slowly and quietly moving forward.

"You okay, Mons? You looked like you had a hard time in there?"

Grant studied Mons' face, which never revealed much about what he was thinking.

"Fine now. Just don't like confined spaces."

Mons shrugged and Grant thought he could see a hint of embarrassment, which, given how little he usually showed, told Grant he was probably mortified. Not liking confined spaces was an unfortunate handicap when working on a space ship. All said, Grant was somewhat impressed Mons had managed to keep that hidden this long.

"We need to get to engineering to run a scan to see where they are," Clarice said quietly.

Most of the sensitive systems were locked to only allow access from specific consoles hardwired into the system unless wider access had been explicitly authorized by the captain, and a physical switch had been toggled in the bridge. Standard security practice, but a pain at times like these as internal scans were part of the restricted systems.

Engineering was just a corridor away, and they got there without incident. They peeked in. Nobody was there, but as they entered, they heard sounds from closer to the front. Clarice went to one of the engineering privileged access workstations and authenticated herself.

She reconfigured the internal scans to make sure nothing would flag on any of the screens if someone was poking around in the bridge.

Grant watched the corridor as Clarice confirmed with the scans there were still two guards in the nose of the ship. While waiting, Clarice configured a private group network for the three of them that would not flag up on any screens in the bridge. She handed Mons and Grant a mobile terminal each.

After waiting about ten minutes, the last two finally left the bridge.

Grant led the way. They found the bridge apparently untouched apart from a few security notices that suggested they'd tried and failed, to get into a few systems.

Finally, they would be able to start preparing to get off ship. Clarice's eyes went black, signaling she was only watching her virtual *screens*—probably preparing her tools for scanning the station.

Grant couldn't help wincing at the thought that she'd had her real eyes replaced. He'd certainly never consider anything that invasive. He absent-mindedly stroked the stump finger on his right hand, his reminder from an explosives accident. He didn't even have a prosthetic put in place for that. Not that he had anything against technology, but he didn't want to be technology.

He did have, and used, contact lens screens when he needed to, such as in flight when the flexibility was critical, but he preferred working on one of the hardwired workstations when he could.

Chapter 23

Mons sat quietly on the bridge, deep in thought, while Clarice was busy preparing the improvements she'd wanted to do to her scans when they were interrupted earlier, and Grant went off to the side to do whatever he was doing on one of the privileged access workstations.

Mons wasn't sure what to do. He liked Captain Ortega, and it was very much in his nature to be loyal and obedient to those whose authority he was under. But he worried this job seemed like it might go off the rails, and he was concerned he might sooner or later find himself in a situation where he'd have to make a choice between the captain and saving himself.

The idea pained him. He liked to think of himself as the type of person who would take a bullet for the right person, and a captain should be that person. He had been very pleased when Captain Ortega took this job. He believed in what Sovereign Earth said about the threat of the Centauri, and when the captain took the job, he felt a sense of pride to serve her.

So he was not pleased they were about to pry instead of just asking about the concerns they had. Of course, this station wasn't technically Sovereign Earth's, but given Terrell clearly represented them somehow, it was close enough for Mons.

He wanted the captain to be reassured without having to do anything that might anger their hosts. He harbored a hope they would get more jobs that would help reveal the danger of the Centauri gate.

He glanced over at Grant.

What is he doing that is taking so long anyway? he thought to himself. Clarice was the one preparing the modified security scan.

It looked like Grant was looking at the communications logs. Mons wondered what he was doing with those. He moved closer and Grant quickly closed them.

"Ready?" he asked.

Mons' eyes narrowed in suspicion, but he didn't let on.

"Yes, as soon as Clarice's scan is ready to go."

Clarice was almost done wrapping up her program when a flash in her peripheral vision alerted her that someone had triggered one of her security alerts. It flagged a comms log access. Her eyes remained blackened but her normal display faded and she accessed a replay of her eye camera, observing Mons sullen on one side of the bridge, and Grant at the console that had been flagged. She couldn't see the screen, but she didn't have to. She could see a data feed from her security probe in the system overlaid on her vision and got a summary of the searches Grant had done.

She was puzzled. He was poking around in private comms he wasn't meant to be accessing. He normally shouldn't even have access—he only did because he was at the privileged access console in the bridge that was unlocked purely because she'd used the appropriate access controls to unlock the bridge terminals for the scans they were about to do.

Just as she was about to dig deeper, she heard Mons ask Grant if he was ready, and Grant saying her name.

She switched her eyes to their normal mode, and smiled, making a mental note to look into Grant's searches later.

"I'm all ready."

She nudged Grant away from the privileged console and loaded her program. It would use the same low-powered scans but in pulses across a much wider band and cross-correlate the results to the composition of materials matched against the public plans. While the public plans were undoubtedly no longer accurate, she hoped they were close enough that she could use them to narrow down the result categories enough to clean up the scan results.

It looked promising. In any case, it was the best they could do. They soon had what at least looked like a much better map, and projected it so they could more easily discuss where to go first.

"Here, this looks like a secondary engineering room, given it's so near one of the power plants. I bet there will be a hardwired console there with elevated access rights."

Clarice pointed at a room not far from where they were docked. It did, however, mean passing through several corridors and past a number of rooms they couldn't be sure whether would be occupied. If they were concerned about security, there'd also be every chance there would be guards in or outside the plant room itself, and possibly the engineering room they were aiming for. If that was even what it was.

The others didn't have any better ideas, though, so they geared up and carefully moved to the entrance.

"If they had any sense," Clarice said, "they would have a physical lock on the docking port."

It was a pet peeve of hers. Everyone relied on electronic door locks. But these electronic locks had next to no real security, because they all had emergency overrides that relied on assumptions about physical access that just did not hold if the person on the other side had adequate equipment.

The point was that anyone who really expected unwanted visitors to be hiding on a ship typically wouldn't let that ship dock. If they did so anyway, they'd do a search. Most of the time, the docking port locks were there to prevent people from entering ships that were not theirs, not to prevent people aboard the ships from entering the station.

Clarice grinned as she effortlessly tricked the docking port's electronic lock into thinking an override had been entered into the keypad, because someone had thought it was a good idea to let the keypad handle the authentication and just send a signal to the lock. Stupid design.

The door slid open. They waited a few seconds in case they'd been heard. There was no sign of anyone. Apparently, the guards were so certain they'd done a thorough enough job that they hadn't even kept anyone stationed there.

Clarice scanned the room with her augments and pointed out the likely cameras. There were only a couple and they wouldn't cover the entire room. She led the way toward the first hallway, crouching just out of view of the cameras.

Chapter 24

Terrell's tour of the station underlined the idea that he wanted to think of himself as a bit of a modern-day Nemo and saw his station as a surrogate for the famed fictional submarine, a voluntary exile from a home he perceived as under the control of enemy forces. Isolated from the mainstream of society, while exploring new frontiers.

The paintings on the walls, in particular, were a mix of what Zo presumed were reproductions, paintings contemporary to the Nemo he had modeled his station on, and modern paintings of space exploration.

None of the crew wanted to challenge their very own Nemo on the fact that his *ship* stayed in the same orbit in one of the most well-traveled, safest, portions of space in the solar system outside Earth orbit, and didn't actually explore anything new.

Terrell took the threat of the Centauri seriously. Zo could tell from the intensity of it when he spoke of them that he was not just a casual supporter of Sovereign Earth, putting in some money.

"We can't survive if we are fighting among ourselves, Captain. We need to strengthen the supremacy of Earth. It's the only way we can build a civilization strong enough to stand up to the Centauri."

Zo nodded along, but didn't answer.

"When—not if—they attack, we need to be ready. That's why this mission was so important. We're not ready. It's absolutely necessary that we buy time to tie this system together into a cohesive whole and use the resources of the whole system to build defenses."

Terrell almost spat the words out.

"And you're absolutely sure they'll attack? They're not just leading the Mars separatists along?"

"You have to understand, Captain, there is an imperative for any such civilization to attack, because otherwise, sooner or later some upstart will attack *them* and they won't be ready."

He hadn't answered her question. Zo wasn't sure whether he realized that he was going in circles or not.

117

"It's why we haven't seen signals from any other civilization, Captain Ortega. Everyone smart keeps radio silence. Avoid attracting attention. *That* is the solution to the Fermi paradox . . . The smart ones hide."

"Since we've already made noise, we need to hole up and become an undesirably expensive target instead."

They talked as they bounced through lavishly decorated rooms and hallways, with more and more replicas of famous paintings and ornate furniture that would have seemed to fit better in a stately manor on Earth than in a space station where they had to be bolted down and fitted with straps. Because the low-perceived gravity was low enough for someone's sudden movement to send them flying across the room.

Zo felt a weird mix of being at ease and on guard at the same time. Terrell was charming and seemed open and forthcoming, but she wasn't sure she believed him when he insisted he knew nothing about the Vanguard attack.

He didn't seem worried enough.

If they were Mars Colony ships as the rumors on the net said, then wouldn't he, with his strong views of Earth supremacy over the colonies, be incensed and concerned?

Terrell took her elbow and gently led her into an observation lounge at the opposite end of the station from the docking port. Unlike Vanguard, which spun too fast, Nautilus' gentle spin made it relatively pleasant to look out the observation window. The lounge was also much larger than Vanguard's because most people spent a couple of minutes out of curiosity in Vanguards' observation lounge and had enough of the rotation, so there was little point in devoting space to it.

According to Terrell, the lounge was loosely modeled on the old Jules Verne restaurant in the Eiffel Tower.

Zo took his word for it, as she had never traveled much on Earth, and never been to Paris.

It was slightly protruding from the rest of the station so there was a 360-degree view to the *sides*, toward the rim of the station and beyond, where the large windows were partially obscured here and there by thick iron lattice

118

columns meant to evoke the Eiffel Tower, while *up* you stared into a large unobstructed observation window that didn't seek to maintain the illusion.

"A concession for the sake of the view. I was of two minds about it, but it makes the space, don't you think?"

It was clear this was Terrell's pride.

Direction made little sense here as they were in the center of rotation of the station and so practically weightless. *Down* in this room was arbitrarily defined by the side where the tables were mounted and the chairs magnetically held in place.

"This is where we'll dine."

Once again, Terrell sounded like he was expecting applause, and Zo had to hold herself back to prevent herself from clapping slowly in a show of sarcasm.

He clearly expected everyone to be impressed, but Zo was not the type to be particularly impressed by wealth. She was more impressed by the extent of vanity he was displaying and wondered how much he had to compensate for. It distracted her for a moment and made her slightly smirk while he resumed talking about the importance of her mission and his other work as she took in the views.

"I hope we can count on you for additional missions, Captain Ortega."

He smiled at her. The closest to a real smile he had exhibited so far, and it made him so much more appealing than all of his flashy vanity had.

If only his demeanor was like that *all the time*, she thought to herself. She smiled back, a bit friendlier, still uncertain, but not wanting to let on.

"I'd be happy to discuss what you have in mind, Mr. Terrell."

"Sebastien, please, I feel we know each other already."

***

The dinner was also clearly intended to soften her up.

Even though transport costs had dropped, and transport times had dropped enough to make fresh food possible this far out, truly fresh food for anyone in the colonies but the super-rich was a rarity.

119

It wasn't that it was hard to get food there fast enough, but it still had to be boosted out of Earth gravity, and then carried through the Earth-Mars gate, and then passed on to Nautilus. And though the gate travel was cheap relative to the immense distances, there were tolls for passage—the extent to which tolls were used to maintain Earth control was one of the big complaints of the colonial governments—and the transport and crew costs needed to get things to and from the gates also added up.

Of course the *Black Rain* crew did travel to Earth space regularly, but they rarely went down to the surface, so fresh Earth food was still not something they ate often.

Mars Colony had started producing some fresh produce and some meat as the dropping costs of dome-building started making domestication and agriculture attractive. But the irony was that almost all of it ended up being exported back to Earth where the exotic nature of even basics like carrots grown in Martian soil—which Zo knew first hand tasted exactly the same—coupled with the still-limited supply and with the sheer weight of the magnitudes larger Earth market had created the bizarre situation that it was more expensive to buy Martian-grown vegetables on Mars than to buy Earth vegetables transported to Mars orbit.

Terrell—Sebastien—was giving them the good stuff. Food fresh enough that he had paid for express transport.

Their dinner probably cost a few dozen times as much as what the crew usually spent on food in a month.

It didn't necessarily make them more likely to believe. But it did make the atmosphere ease up. The crew were clearly enjoying themselves, and Zo felt sorry for Clarice, Mons, and Grant, whom she'd left behind on the ship. Grant mostly—Clarice and Mons were nothing alike, but they shared a lack of appreciation for eating as a pleasure and both seemed to treat it as a pointless activity keeping them from more interesting endeavors.

On the other hand, if they found nothing wrong, maybe they'd take more jobs for Terrell and get to dine here again.

Maybe they *had* been wrong.

During the meal Zo kept gently probing Terrell for hints he knew more than he let on, and Terrell kept gently but consistently nudging her onto lighter topics. Maybe he was hiding something, or maybe he just didn't want to talk shop during dinner.

Her mind went back and forth.

Zo hoped Clarice was having better luck, whether it'd implicate or clear their host.

Chapter 25

"Hold on, let's wait for a bit and keep an eye on the guards. With some luck, they're equally sloppy about staying at their posts . . . Wouldn't do us any harm if we're able to get off without having to *disappear* any guards this early."

Two guards were blocking their path, chatting, with their backs to them, but right next to the door they needed to enter. They were clearly not paying much attention, but they'd certainly notice if someone tried to open the door while they were there.

Clarice was in the lead, and patiently observing the men, hoping for them to move, but they stayed there, talked, wandered about a little bit, and talked some more. They could hear bits and pieces of their conversation, but nothing interesting.

Clarice was getting worried it'd take too long, and started reviewing her scans, looking for another way to their target when they got lucky.

A shift change, and the idiots went to get their relief rather than get them on comms or wait at their posts. Grant grinned at Clarice.

"Okay, this is it."

They moved quickly, worried the replacements might get there while they were still fumbling with the door. Thankfully, the door was unlocked and they got into a second, smaller bank of docking ports, with a number of hallways leading off it.

They spread out to check the hallways and match them to the scans and quickly found the right one. They couldn't hear anyone. If they were right, they were almost there. They were about to turn into the next corridor when they heard voices and bounced as quietly and rapidly as they could back down the corridor and back into the smaller docking area.

The voice kept coming closer, and Clarice, on impulse, tried the hatch to one of the smaller ships. It was open, and she motioned for the others to enter.

"Hope nobody is home . . ."

They got lucky—it was a tiny shuttle, probably just used between Nautilus and other stations in Mars space. They kept the hatch ajar and listened to the voices outside. Just maintenance staff complaining about their work.

Clarice looked around to see if there was anything interesting in the ship while they were there, but didn't dare touch any controls in case they set off any alarms, and found nothing.

The maintenance people soon moved on, and Clarice led them back out and down the corridor they'd been in. This time there were no other people, and they turned into the next corridor and started looking for the right door to the room they'd identified.

The first two doors were locked. The third one was open, but just led to an office with no fixed terminal. The fourth likewise.

"It must be one of the locked ones. Typical."

The locks on these doors were nowhere near as ineffective as the ones on the docking port. Clearly they did care about keeping people out of these rooms. They might have to let Grant have a go with his explosives . . . Clarice wasn't happy about that. She disliked the idea of something that couldn't be achieved with intellect alone in the first place, and more importantly, even a tiny little targeted explosion was likely to attract attention.

She probed the lock for weaknesses and eventually found one. The lock was magnetic. As long as it had power, it'd remain locked unless a signal from the security system told it to shut down. This was a basic concession between security and safety: if the power went, the door would unlock automatically as a failsafe, ensuring anyone inside would be able to get out in an emergency.

Clarice first tried to find a way to feed the locking mechanism the unlock signal, but this door didn't suffer from a technically incompetent software developer like the docking port. She had to look for a hardware weakness. Her infrared sight showed a possible weakness—a component she might be able to overload and burn out by wedging a thin wire through a slight gap where the casing was bolted onto the door.

The first attempt failed—the wire got stuck. Grant helped wedge the gap open a bit more with a screwdriver, and Clarice got it far enough in. She grabbed an electric stun gun from her tool bag. She attached the other end of the wire and turned on the electricity. The wire melted in seconds and left a charred mark around the lock. Smoke smelling of melting metal and burning plastic rose from the lock, and they heard just a little pop as it short-circuited and power to the locking mechanism failed.

"Hurry. Chances are a warning light or alarm might have gone off. Let's check if it's the right place and then find a hiding place to wait."

They all looked through what was, in fact, a secondary engineering room. There were multiple consoles there, and they checked each in turn.

"Here."

Mons had found one that appeared to have privileged access. Clarice checked it and probed the security to make sure it was what they needed.

"Hurry, I think I can hear voices."

Grant was keeping an eye on the corridor.

"Okay, this will do."

Clarice was pleased. The workstation appeared to have almost unrestricted access. In theory, at least. She'd first need to be able to probe it. She took out a hardware device from her bag and quickly adhered a thin film over the touch screen of the workstation, with a flat cable connecting to the tiny device she attached to the back of the console.

They hurried out, closed the door, and went to one of the unlocked offices, and hid as best they could.

They could hear the guards check the door and argue about what had happened. After checking inside and not noticing Clarice's device, one stayed behind while the other went to get maintenance. It sounded like they believed it was just an accidental burnout.

Clarice's eyeballs went black as she linked up with the device she left behind—a very simple device that mixed a grid of CCD camera sensors with the ability to trigger the capacitive touch screen just as if you were standing in front of the device, combined with a network interface.

It was a convenient and crude way of bridging an airgap to a hardwired console. The data stream could be transmitted to a tablet and effectively mirror the display and touch, but Clarice preferred to have the screen projected, and sensors in the gloves she used let her manipulate the display with *virtual hands*.

I have to get integrated sensors, she thought to herself—the gloves were annoying. Subcutaneous sensors in her fingertips were next on her list of augmentations. She'd excitedly, and with a wink, told Zo how great it'd be to be able to transmit the sensation of touching someone at a distance, but Zo hadn't shared her excitement.

The terminal in the secondary engineering room sprung to life as Clarice started poking and prodding the system, looking for a suitable weakness.

Chapter 26

Terrell kept alternating between telling them all stories about various exploits, sports, numerous adventures, and business, getting the crew more and more off guard in Zo's opinion, and talking to her about what he hoped to achieve.

"You've not really lived if you haven't been to the top of Olympus Mons," he told her. She didn't argue with him, but she found his insistence of bragging about Olympus Mons another indicator of his nature of exaggeration—she knew full well that the gradual slopes of Olympus stretched past the horizon, and as a result, the impression of height is much diminished. And while big, its caldera was no deeper than Pavonis Mons where Tharsis was located.

"Standing there, at the highest peak in the solar system. You can't match it!"

It struck Zo that he was all about symbolism and signaling. The top of Olympus Mons mattered most purely because it was tallest, even though the view was not that impressive.

She exchanged a couple of glances with Vincent, who, true to his nature, was still calm and alert, just barely sipping the wine on offer, and clearly not taken in. Sebastien seemed genuine, but both Vincent and Zo were skeptical creatures.

Zo touched a barely noticeable sensor—if Clarice had something, or was caught, she'd break radio silence, not before, but they'd configured a very low power channel, just enough to send a *ping* to confirm they were okay and ask for one back. It was simple enough, and by design noisy enough, that it shouldn't be picked up even if station security was monitoring comms traffic.

She got a *ping* back after a few seconds. It didn't tell her much, but it did tell her Clarice and her team were still fine.

Sebastien was telling her about the gains Sovereign Earth was making on Earth. How they might even win the next elections. He was excited.

"What we have is an opportunity to truly reshape the system," he said.

"Instead of that blasted Centauri crap, we can focus on fully exploiting the solar system. There's so much we've not done yet. Resource extraction from Jupiter is only just starting. We're only returning the smallest of asteroids from the belt."

Terrell's eyes glowed and twinkled.

"As long as we can stop that blasted gate, then by the time the Centauri tries coming here the long way, we'll have refined the gate tech so much we can throw whole asteroids at an incoming force. We'll show them what Earth ingenuity can do with their toys."

Zo nodded. As much as she was worried about the Centauri too, Sebastien seemed like he almost relished the prospect of an arms race with them.

"All we need is *will to power*. The will to stand up to the colonies and show them we're stronger together."

Zo shivered.

That phrase, she thought to herself. She knew what it represented. Where it came from. Nietzsche. She hoped that was where Terrell had drawn it from, because the alternatives, the movements that had made it their own later, were far worse.

Terrell beamed at her. His broad smile and eyes glinting with excitement.

"Once we take down the Mars separatists, the colony will accept it needs us. When the Mars separatists fall, all the colonies will fall back into line."

Zo got more uncomfortable. *Falling back into line* and this *will to power* crap sounded a bit authoritarian for her tastes. She just wanted to be able to keep flying without being hassled by military ships all the time and without worrying about what the gate would bring.

She didn't really care who had the final say on Mars or in the colonies all that much.

Zo pinged Clarice again. She got two pings back this time. As agreed, this meant they were working to get into the station systems.

She turned toward Terrell and tried changing the subject.

"What do you for fun around here?" she asked while raising her wineglass.

"Wouldn't you like to know."

127

When she didn't think Terrell could get any more cheesy, he took her hand and uttered that, "My parties are legendary . . . I'll make sure you get an invite. A woman such as yourself would be . . . very popular."

The hair on Zo's forearms rose. She could think of fewer things she wanted less than to be popular at a party arranged by Terrell.

She regretted asking even more as Terrell launched into a detailed description of his parties, including too much detail of his sexual exploits—another thing he seemed a bit too proud of.

But at least he soon turned toward Rob on his other side to seek additional approval of his multiple partners.

Rob looked uncomfortable and Zo winked at him and shrugged, happy for temporary relief and perfectly fine with throwing Rob to the wolves for the time being.

Chapter 27

Grant was squatting near the door, his eyes and ears firmly on the corridor while Mons and Clarice hid behind the desk as Clarice tried to hack into the station systems. He didn't want to interrupt and didn't want to cause any sounds, even though was dying to ask how she was getting along.

The person from maintenance had just arrived to fix the door of the engineering room down the corridor, and the guard was still there, waiting impatiently for him to finish.

Grant couldn't see much as he didn't dare open the door a lot, but he could hear the maintenance person complain about how in the world the circuitry could have melted so totally. He was forced to remove and replace the whole thing.

Soon he disappeared, going to fetch a new lock assembly.

The guard took to pacing up and down the corridor while waiting, and Grant let the door slide shut and sidled up to Mons.

"How is she doing?" he whispered.

"How would I know?" Mons answered and shrugged passively.

"I can hear you, you know," Clarice responded. "I've found a weakness, but it's a bit of a pain to exploit. Patience."

Grant moved quietly back to the door. He must not have been careful enough, because he nudged the desk, and the motion must have knocked over something on it. In the low gravity it was flying in what seemed like slow motion toward the wall and bounced against it, giving off a weak thud as it did.

It was some stupid decorative figurine. Grant caught it before it hit the floor. But that little thud of it bouncing off the wall was enough. He could hear the guard stop and move up to the door.

He motioned to Mons to get ready on one side of the door while he was on the other, waiting for the guard to enter. Hopefully, he had decided to just investigate on his own instead of calling it in.

The door slid open, and the guard spent a couple of seconds looking around, and turned and looked into Grant's face just as Grant set off Clarice's stun gun. The man fell to the ground, shaking, foam coming from his mouth. He tried reaching for his comms to trigger an alarm, but Grant grabbed the comms unit and smashed it. The man kept spasming after the gun stopped and eventually went limp.

"Did you kill him?" Mons asked.

Grant didn't think so. The stun guns were usually very safe, but the man had gone down unusually quickly, so Grant checked his pulse anyway.

"He should be fine."

They grabbed tie strips from Clarice's bag and tied his arms and legs together. Grant looked around for something to use as a gag and found nothing. He ended up tearing one sleeve off the guard's uniform, stuffed it in the guard's mouth, and fastened that too with tie strips.

He'd probably be able to wiggle and get the gag out with enough time, but once they left, they only needed enough time to make their escape anyway, and in any case, this put them on a severe time constraint—it wouldn't take long before someone in security would wonder where he was.

He explained what had gone down to Clarice, who coolly pointed out she could hear, and her alert system had brought up an infrared view when no motion was visible from behind the desk.

Sometimes Grant thought Clarice seemed more machine than human, even though he had seen her sensitive side as well. He was a very empathetic man and felt he could never understand how Clarice seemed to be able to just turn her emotions on and off at will like that.

Grant went back to checking the doorway to make sure the brief fight hadn't attracted any attention. No signs of any guards. The maintenance man came back with the new lock assembly, and seemed puzzled not to see the guard, but quickly went to work.

He'd done all the preparations, so it took him just a few minutes to bolt the new lock in place and test it before he shuffled off down the corridor.

Chapter 28

Jonas was sitting opposite Zo and Terrell, next to Vincent. He observed closely. It worried him that it seemed like Zo got along so well with Terrell. He didn't trust the man. Seemed too eager and too sure of himself, which might not be real indications of trouble, but it made Jonas instinctively dislike him. Jonas always disliked people who puffed themselves up.

There might well be some jealousy too, he thought. The station was incredible, though gaudy. And Zo was an attractive woman. He almost blushed for thinking about his captain that way.

"What do you think?"

Vincent was whispering into his ear.

"I don't like him, but I've not seen anything directly wrong." Jonas tried to be objective.

"He's just given us the tourist view, though."

Jonas gave a small nod. It was true. They'd been shown *the sights*. The bridge, the observation deck, the trading posts, and communal areas open to a limited set of traders Terrell favored, dealing in goods he personally enjoyed as well as some he merely made a big profit off. He'd more than hinted there was an expansive trade in drugs on the station, though he didn't openly admit it. No laws were broken out here, but his customers would appreciate discretion to make their passage through Earth or Mars customs easier.

He'd not shown them anything operational—the bridge was sanitized; in that it clearly only housed the station-keeping staff. No command staff involved in any Sovereign Earth business, if any, were on this station. No one else that seemed like they might be crews for hire like the *Black Rain*. No smoke-filled back room where conspiratorial meetings took place.

Of course, the reason he didn't show any of that might be that nothing like that was going on here. He could just be providing funds like he said and hosting little recruitment drives like this.

They might be here just because this wasn't somewhere important to Sovereign Earth, and Earth security was unlikely to look for the Vanguard thieves here.

It troubled Jonas that he seemed to take things so lightly, though. They'd handed over the capsule, although he was unaware they'd made a copy of the data. So why hadn't his crew run off to a comms room somewhere and ensured it was decrypted and then spread to every news channel in the system to reveal the invasion plans they'd been told were on there? Or even to verify the contents.

He explained this concern to Vincent in short, whispered sentences through clenched teeth while nodding and smiling to Terrell, who told another one of his vanity anecdotes.

Vincent nodded.

Neither of them was the type to hold long discussions about subjects like these. Their backgrounds were different, but they were both fighters who understood the value of being concise and precise.

There were several alternatives, Jonas mused. Terrell might simply be the simple playboy he tried to portray, someone who genuinely didn't find it interesting enough and who left following up the storage device to others, though he also seemed to get very animated about Sovereign Earth's goals, so that didn't seem to quite fit.

He might not be that important, and knew he'd done his part in obtaining the capsule, get it copied, which he might have done when he checked it, and getting the original brought to safety as evidence in due time.

Maybe Sovereign Earth would use this to push the government into concessions rather than outright release it. Jonas detested this kind of backhanded politics. He just wished they'd broadcast the whole thing and deal with the fallout.

Chapter 29

Clarice's progress with the station systems was slow at first. She methodically probed to look for weaknesses. She had access to basic internal systems without any credentials, because the system designer had foolishly assumed that since she had physical access to the terminal, behind a door that should require access control, the user could be trusted.

But these were only low-security systems that anyone with access to the room could be trusted with, such as environmental controls within safe parameters, and internal comms and unprivileged information lookups.

The latter was her first avenue of attack. She rapidly searched through the unprivileged information about the station and had her computer index everything she looked through. One of the things she found was public employee records for the station. Not much detail, but photos, names, and usernames for everyone. Usernames would be useful.

She kept probing for more information, looking for anything that would give her hints to guess at passwords, or find other holes. She worked at practically a superhuman speed—she didn't need to read the contents of the pages as her computer system indexed and condensed everything, flagged things worth slowing down to ingest, and she didn't need to type out most commands. Once in a new system she *showed* her system how to navigate the system at first then had it repeat it as fast as the interface allowed while scanning the pages.

In the background, her programs built up a map of relationships between the pieces of information gleaned. She came across internal discussion forums, and the profiles of staff members expanded rapidly. Family members mentioned in discussions. Names of old partners. Birth dates of children.

In addition to the data for password guesses, she recorded any mention of Sovereign Earth or comings and goings of people on the station for future analysis.

Soon she had enough to try probing for some passwords. A handful of people who had, over the last couple of years, given up a scrap of information here and there that some basic statistics suggested she ought to find a password among.

The password scan was slower than hoped—the system added delays after each failure, but thankfully only per user. But she only dared have the system test two attempts per user, for now, to avoid blocking accounts and triggering alerts.

She got one password, but only for a low-level employee in the kitchen.

It was a start, however. It gave access to a few new systems.

Staff rosters, which let her augment her model with who spent time with whom to correlate against mentions of partners and other discussions.

And staff had access to logs of visitors. Clarice quickly grabbed all she could of those. She cross-matched names of visitors with names of station staff, and finally, she got lucky.

A careless Lt. Cameron in security posted about his daughter's birthday two years ago and mentioned her birthday. The visitor logs showed he regularly had two female visitors with his last name. Only one of them ever came alone. Clarice surmised the one who came alone was probably his wife, the other likely their daughter.

She got lucky on the second combination of the daughter's name and birthdate. She tutted to herself. A security officer should know better. But these were people who didn't understand computer security, they were there for the physical, hands-on stuff.

Clarice smiled to herself when she saw what Lt. Cameron had access to.

"I'm in," she whispered to Grant and Mons, as she rapidly went through the security logs, and scanned through recording after recording.

The system, very helpfully, had a suitably fancy facial detection system that automatically tagged images and allowed searches by tag, allowing her to focus on recordings with Terrell in them.

Either Terrell didn't understand that his security system allowed his staff to keep him under surveillance too, or he was the type who enjoyed having anything he did also covered, in case he needed a recording of whomever he was with later.

Clarice soon had her system indexing and captioning speech in all the videos it found of him, and it started indexing terms in the conversations.

Most of it was boring stuff. Staff problems. Terrell trying to seduce an endless stream of women, and a few men, and succeeding in doing so often enough to keep him busy—he did so with a disturbingly rehearsed set of stories. Commercial arrangements.

She was starting to think she'd not find anything interesting when the first Sovereign Earth related conversation was flagged. The conversation itself wasn't very interesting per se. It was someone briefly thanking Terrell for having introduced someone to the *cause*. But it helped link two other people to Sovereign Earth, and suddenly Clarice's interface flagged a cluster of people that had interacted with both Terrell and one or both of the people involved.

As a result, a number of other videos soon popped up, including conversations that standing alone seemed innocuous, but in light of knowing both parties involved were likely involved in Sovereign Earth, gave additional scraps of information.

The map of conversations and people grew rapidly from that, and Clarice had to go through and narrow down the search parameters to prioritize what to scan for.

A handful of people seemed central to the cluster of possible Sovereign Earth contacts she found. She wondered if they might be part of the leadership, or just Terrell's contacts. They mostly discussed logistics.

Some of it involved ship purchases and other transactions that suggested they were certainly doing more than politics.

Suddenly a mention of Vanguard popped up. And a mention of the gate. They didn't say much. Just mentioned a project. But the conversations helped add an additional two people to the network to search for, and provided a focus to prioritize the now very long list of conversations to go through.

"I think I have something," she whispered.

"About time." Mons was unhappy they were digging into this in the first place, and being hidden away in this office wondering when a guard might walk in had made him more sullen than usual.

Clarice ignored him.

She'd found two recordings with the same group of three people. Terrell and two people not mentioned by name. The first discussed *work on the gate*

135

a few months ago. The second discussed *the Vanguard project* a couple of days before Zo had been approached.

"Shit. Shit. Shit. You have to watch these."

Clarice grabbed a tiny device from her bag and projected the videos onto the wall for Grant and Mons to see.

Chapter 30

"Welcome, gentlemen."

Terrell beamed at his two visitors.

"How was the trip?"

"Excellent," man number one answered, while grabbing Terrell's hand.

The other extended his hand to Terrell too, and they sat down in his office.

"We have good news."

Man number one was leaning back as he spoke. Terrell offered them both drinks and they eagerly accepted, presumably having enjoyed Terrell's rather expensive tastes before.

"Our agent is in. His comms are severely limited due to security, but he can get short messages out. He is confident he can get the data we need on the gate."

"That is good news. Will it be enough to achieve what we need?" Terrell asked, leaning in and looking animated.

"He thinks so. His latest message suggests that he can get hold of a quantum encryption module that will allow us to inject gate commands that will validate."

"The module he's there to work on has sufficiently high-level access that he's been able to sneak in a backdoor we can trigger once his module has been installed. It should give us access to systems at the top clearance level."

"Sounds promising. Were my blueprints useful?"

Terrell looked pleased with himself.

"Yes, very. Buying the company that supplies the defensive systems for the gate was a masterstroke," the second man said. This was the first time the second man had spoken.

"The specifications and blueprints show we should be able to inject commands to the weapons systems, triggering a cascading overload. If we time it right, the whole thing will blow."

"We better time it right then."

"We should be able to use it to trigger the overload during the final phase of construction after the quantum core is installed. Of course, there are the backup cores, but it'll buy us several years while they rebuild, and it'll be one down, two cores to go, before the gate is useless until new counterpart cores can be sent sublight to the Centauri system."

Terrell grinned. From there on, the conversation trailed off into details that were not particularly pertinent.

***

Grant looked shocked. Mons seemed deep in thought. The recording was consistent to an extent with what they knew: Sovereign Earth desperately wanted to prevent the gate from coming online. Clarice also had to admit that if they were right and there was an invasion planned, then blowing up the gate if there was no other alternative didn't seem all that bad. She'd thought, after seeing the first recording, that it wasn't in itself a deal-breaker for her, though it meant they'd been lied to, and Zo would need to know.

"Let's see the second recording."

Clarice brought up the second one, taken much more recently, though the scene was almost identical at first, with Terrell welcoming the same two men.

***

"We've had no luck getting the capsule released from Vanguard, so we'll need to proceed, Mr. Terrell."

"I thought as much. I've prepared a couple of options. Our man has nothing Sovereign Earth related on him, right? Nobody would be that stupid, right?"

"Of course not."

"Good. Just checking." Terrell smiled slightly and brought up a projection.

"These are our newest toys."

138

The projection showed two large colonial cruisers with Mars Colony emblems on them.

"I had hoped we could use them for something else, but we can still hit a two-in-one this way. Got more of these coming anyway."

Terrell waited for dramatic effect and enjoyed watching his guests lean forward.

"I've found the perfect crew to attempt to retrieve the capsule. I have a good feeling they'll succeed. We've prepped a story about Mars insurrectionists working with the Centauri for a coordinated attack. We all understand the danger of the Centauri, but it's easier to sell it quickly this way."

Terrell lifted his hands, palms up, in an apologetic gesture.

"The cruisers will serve two very useful purposes: If my hired hands get captured, they'll undoubtedly give up the information we've given them sooner or later. Their story of Mars insurrectionists will fit perfectly with the Mars Colony emblems on the cruisers that will attack Vanguard."

The two men gasped.

"You're going to attack Vanguard? It's suicide."

"Well, none of us are going to be on the ships. I have crews willing and ready. If they get away that'd be great, but if not . . . What can you do?"

He didn't wait for an answer.

"The important thing is that whether my hired hands succeed or not, Mars takes the blame and nobody will be looking to us."

"With some luck, the government will rein Mars in *and* we'll get the quantum encryption module we need."

***

Clarice turned off the display. Grant looked stunned. Mons just looked confused and sullen, but that was so close to how he always looked, Clarice didn't know how to process it.

"We need to alert the captain right away."

Mons was getting unusually animated as the content of the clip was sinking in.

"We need to stop them. They're trying to start a damn war on the back of a damn lie!"

Clarice had never seen Mons look this angry before, but she understood him. She was seething herself, though she barely showed it.

She nodded, and *pinged* Zo three times, to signal they had something important and were about to do a transmission that might be noticed.

Chapter 31

Zo asked for the bathroom and excused herself so she'd be somewhere private when Clarice sent whatever data she'd found. Her disguised comm unit sprung to life shortly after she'd entered the bathroom, and she quietly watched the clips on her contact screen.

The first clip felt understandable. It might be a fallback, she thought to herself. If they knew about the attack and had no other options, maybe it'd be the right thing to do. It could save billions of lives.

She watched the second clip with some trepidation. Her lips soon pursed, and she could feel her face heat up.

Terrell had lied to her! The weasel had promised he knew nothing about the Vanguard attack, and all the time he was behind it. He was prepared to cause a war with Mars on false pretenses.

And he was going to destroy the gate on no evidence at all, just fear.

She suddenly felt very stupid and used. She'd not asked for any evidence—she was so ready to believe the story he told at first. Even when his personality repulsed her, she kept telling herself to separate his personality from the *cause*.

Clearly she didn't particularly trust the Mars Colony and had fears about the Centauri sufficient enough that when someone painted a picture of them working together to threaten Earth, she was all too willing to just blindly believe it without any kind of verification.

She wasn't the type to swear, but a stream of expletives suddenly came in quick succession.

They'd made themselves into fugitives for this.

She focused on her breathing, trying to calm down, because she knew there was a much more immediate problem.

If Terrell was willing to risk their lives by attacking Vanguard right as they were breaking in, and willing to start a war with Mars, and willing to kill the construction crews on the gate over a fear held without evidence, she was suddenly certain he wouldn't hesitate to murder her and her crew if he thought they were a liability.

It explained the expensive meal and the spectacle he was making of himself and his cause. He wanted them alive, but if he wasn't convinced he'd sold them on Sovereign Earth by the end of it, they'd be unlikely to get off the station.

She felt betrayed. Angry, but also sad that he had stolen a purpose away from her. She had been softening, wondering if maybe they should take on more missions. Help stop an invasion. Save the system. Save humanity. Do something more with their lives than just be a glorified delivery service.

She quite liked the idea of being a hero.

It's all a fucking lie, she thought to herself.

A knot grew in Zo's stomach and her entire body tightened like a cornered animal ready to pounce and tear its attacker apart.

They weren't just going to escape, but take this bastard down and reveal his whole shady scheme.

But first, she'd need to calm down and get back to Terrell and get through dinner without exploding in his face and revealing everything. On the contrary, she needed to be more interested and see how much information she could get out of the piece of shit.

***

It took her a few minutes to compose herself enough to go back out. As she approached Terrell, she caught Jonas' eyes with a look of fury and slid a finger across her throat before looking back down on Terrell.

She was sure she looked crazy to Jonas, before putting on a smile and sitting down again, but she knew Jonas would understand she'd gotten information, and would follow her lead without hesitation even before he knew what she had.

She apologized to Terrell and asked him what they'd been talking about.

Terrell launched straight into his sales pitch again, and this time she listened intently, and started asking questions.

"So, Sebastien, you pretend to be only providing some funding, but you're dealing with us, and I can tell how much the cause means to you. Are you sure you're only the money bags?"

142

She awkwardly slid a hand through her hair, trying to look seductive. It wasn't her style, and she was not confident she was doing it well.

Terrell coyly admitted he might have been underselling his role slightly. He leaned toward her and whispered in her ear.

"Well . . . Sovereign Earth are all friends of mine, if you know what I mean."

"I hear nobody knows who the leader is?" Zo asked.

"That's true. It's meant to be a collective board without one, but everyone is speculating there's a single person at the top, of course."

"Is there?"

"I won't deny that . . . But I won't confirm anything either, Captain; that would be telling."

"And it's well above your pay grade."

"Still."

Terrell looked delighted his audience was now more engaged, but clearly not about to spill secrets that easily.

He seemed to relish the opportunity to draw Zo in further, though.

Chapter 32

"I'd love to be able to tell you more about Sovereign Earth, Captain, but that would require more of a . . . commitment from you and your crew first. I'm sure you understand."

Terrell put his hand on hers and smiled, before quickly withdrawing it and touching it to his ear.

Zo instantly tensed up, worrying it was about their team or that the transfer she received had been noticed.

"I have some serious news, I'm afraid."

Terrell's voice had changed; it was now cold and steely, but not threatening.

"That was my station XO. They've picked up a message saying you're wanted for questioning. No word on whether they suspect you, but it's not great. With respect to my proposal to have you carry out further work, it stands. We're certainly not about to hand you over given what you've done. We can hide you."

He looked at her.

"There are some . . . other locations you can lie low in. And given your ident has been changed already, I can tell you're prepared."

Zo nodded, but avoided voicing an agreement.

"We'll still need to think about it, Sebastien," she said with a smile. "But it is a generous offer."

She tried her very hardest to appear as if she had pretty much bought into his ideas, and as if she didn't know what she had learned.

Terrell softened, his smile returned, and the furrow between his brows disappeared.

"Let's talk more business later. For now, more drinks!"

He motioned to his server.

They talked about Zo's past. She told him the story of how she became captain, and where most saw the implied threat and went quiet, Terrell laughed and complimented her on the fine job.

That made Zo just more certain they needed to stop him—to her that story was both a caution to people not to cross her, but also a reminder to herself that she'd go to any length to defend or avenge her crew, even when it'd leave her with nightmares of her own ability to turn into a savage killer for years afterwards.

Someone who found it funny wasn't someone she wanted to know.

She struggled to appear cheerful while she thought through their options. The first step was obviously going to have to be to get off the station. Ideally, with the *storage unit* she now knew had to contain the quantum encryption core they'd talked about, but worst case they could do without. They had the clips and the data on the unit. The clips ought to be enough evidence for Earth to take Nautilus and capture whatever data they could find. Even if the unit wasn't recaptured, the gate command authentication system could be replaced to prevent it from being usable.

But, if they couldn't get off the station without being found out, none of that would matter. Thankfully, Terrell seemed intent on recruiting them, and Zo was leaning toward accepting to buy time. Maybe resist a bit more, then offer to carry out another operation while seeming open to talking more later—she didn't think Terrell would buy it if she was suddenly eager.

Then, when they were off on another mission, they'd get sufficient distance and transmit the evidence to the government. No, broadcast it. Who knows who they could trust.

But first things first. Zo turned to Terrell to suggest another mission.

Chapter 33

Grant motioned for Clarice and Mons to follow as soon as he'd checked the coast was clear. They'd transferred the files to the captain and were headed back to the ship to get it ready in case they needed to leave in a hurry.

They rushed down the corridor and were back in the second docking area when someone started yelling behind them.

"Oi! You there! Stop!"

A warning shot was fired above their heads. They jumped over some crates and drew their own weapons.

"Come out and we won't shoot."

Grant didn't trust them for a second and fired where the voice was coming from. His shot was met with a series of blasts back.

"They'll have reinforcements here soon. We can't sit here."

"See those handles? Hold on tight, I'm going to blow that docking port."

Grant pointed to a docking port with no ship attached. It was a high-risk gamble to distract their attackers, hoping they'd fall back before the safety doors shut. The problem being they'd be stuck on the wrong side as the docking area would be sealed.

But he didn't wait and threw a grenade.

"What the hell?" they heard one of the guards yelling just before the grenade went off and the air pressure dropped rapidly. It felt like a strong wind, but contained by the limited air volume that could pass through the corridors as the pressure started equalizing, and quickly dropping in speed as the station doors started shutting automatically.

Alarms went off and, as expected, the guards ran for the safety doors, terrified of being left on the wrong side.

"There!"

Grant pointed at the shuttle they'd hid in earlier and they ran to it. It was still unlocked. Once inside, they tried desperately to get it started and get the airlock sealed, but they couldn't get past the security.

"Emergency suits and oxygen over here," Mons yelled.

They got the suits on in a hurry, just as they started gasping for air.

With the suits on and unable to get the shuttle started, Grant motioned to the others and bolted for the hole in the docking port.

He positioned himself along the outside of the shuttle they'd just been in and *jumped* sideways several meters across the docking area until he could grab hold of a ledge on the other side.

The docking areas weren't fully separated on the outside. The ships were locked in place about thirty meters *inside* the outer ring, and halfway out there was a wide doorway between them.

Grant pointed at it and started pulling his way toward it. He was hoping they could go through, get to *Black Rain*, and climb in one of the exterior hatches.

With some luck, without getting shot at.

They made it to the doorway, through it, and Grant pulled himself around the rim until he was near enough *Black Rain* to make a jump for it. He made it across and grabbed hold of a junction box, and started pulling himself in when he lost his grip and bounced back as he reached for it again.

He made a second attempt and this time got a better grip. He moved along the hull until he got to one of the outer access hatches, and opened it. Inside was rope and a lightweight winch. He threw the rope to Mons and hauled both Mons and Clarice inside.

It felt like the airlock took hours to equalize pressure and open the door, and they bounced as fast as they could down along the hallways—Grant to the armory and Clarice and Mons to the bridge.

Grant caught up with them on the bridge, armed with three heavy plasma rifles, and handed Clarice and Mons one each before he went to secure the doors.

Before he was even out of the bridge, he was hit over the head with the back of a gun. Clarice and Mons found themselves facing four guards with guns pointed at them before they were able to raise their own.

Chapter 34

Clarice was dragged into the observation lounge first.

"Zo!"

Zo turned and her smiled quickly disappeared from her face.

"Clarice!"

She turned to Terrell as her face hardened and her lips curled up into a snarl.

"What the hell is this!"

She seemed like she was about to lunge at him, when a guard started moving towards her.

Terrell made a motion for him to hold back.

"I'm confident you know perfectly well what this is, Captain Ortega. Three people it appears you know were found sneaking around the station even though I was assured you informed me of your full crew."

There were too many guards around for them to have a chance to do anything right now. Clarice could see it and she was sure Zo did too, as she quickly settled back down.

"Lieutenant, brief me, please. You can do it in front of these people."

One of the guards stepped forwards.

"Sir, we caught them in the docking area. They blew out a docking port to try to escape by making it onto *Black Rain*. The damage has been repaired."

"We subsequently scanned the security footage and traced them to the secondary engineering room. A technician checked the room and found a console relay device. Checking logs suggests they managed to get into the system and were scanning security logs."

Terrell raised an eyebrow.

"So, tell me . . . Clarice, was it . . . Did you find anything interesting?"

Clarice was scanning the room as best she could with her eyes, looking for a tactical advantage, but nothing obvious stood out. Second best was keeping attention on her and assuming the others were looking for openings too.

"I found out you're a lying piece of shit scumbag . . ."

Terrell grinned.

"What a rude way to talk to someone you haven't even been introduced to."

"I know who you are. Sebastien Terrell. Traitor. Liar. Terrorist."

A guard slapped her.

"No, no, let her talk, I find it amusing. Maybe if you could be more specific?"

Clarice looked at Zo for a hint on whether she wanted Clarice to hold back, or if talking about their find was okay. Zo gave a barely perceptible nod, but Clarice saw it clearly. She also could see, thanks to her augmented eyes, how Zo's every muscle was tense and how her face was boiling with anger despite her dark olive complexion masking much of the redness.

Zo had once said to Clarice that she found her eyes intimidating because she could almost literally see through her.

"We found recordings of you discussing your plans for a terrorist attack on the gate."

The look on Terrell's face suggested he hadn't expected that. His face was starting to turn red too, and on him, it was showing brightly.

"But if what your goons said before was true, we might have come to accept that even though you lied about our mission . . ."

Clarice paused briefly for impact.

"That was until we found a recording of you describing faking the supposed *Mars attack* on Vanguard."

She was literally spitting the last phrase. She was secretly wishing she'd been close enough to Terrell that he'd directly felt the words.

But he looked like he felt them anyway. At least he was getting angry they'd found the clips.

"We sent copies off station."

It was a lie, of course. They'd not been able to send any comms, but Clarice hoped the lie might buy them some time for Terrell to try to verify whether there was anything to it. Make him hesitant to kill them, at least.

She had full trust in Zo. And in Vincent, and Jonas. One of them would figure something out. She had less faith in Rob and Grant in a situation like this, though Grant, at least, would be useful once they were loose and in a

149

fight. Once he woke up, that is—the guards had knocked him unconscious when they were captured.

She had no faith whatsoever in Mons, who had somehow gotten the guard to let him sit in a resigned heap on the floor.

She grinned, hoping to antagonize Terrell further.

"I'm sure both Earth and Mars governments will find it very interesting."

"You're lying."

Terrell sounded pretty sure, but Clarice thought she saw some hints of uncertainty in the way the sides of his lips were shaking as he was gritting his teeth.

More importantly, he kept talking, which suggested she'd at least rattled him.

"We detected a weak transmission earlier. Probably to someone in this room. But we'd definitely have picked up any off station transfers."

"So you think, but we left behind a buoy about a quarter of the way from here to Deimos Guardian. It let us reconfigure the ship to relay that message you intercepted by a narrow, low energy microwave connection. Can't blame you for missing it."

Clarice smiled calmly. It was a total fabrication, but from the way she could see one of the guards slipping out of the room, it was clear someone would spend some time looking very thoroughly into if there was any way her story could be true.

It was theoretically plausible they could have gotten away with that, she thought, and half wished they'd tried. Or even just rigged up a transmitter to make it look like they'd done it.

Next time, she told herself.

She looked around the room, and let her eyes scan everything in as much detail as possible. She was functionally blind while she went through the replay in detail, zoomed in, and switched spectrum. She quickly had a detailed assessment of the room, but nothing that helped much. All the guards carried weapons. There was nothing else in the room that seemed like it could help them—the deadliest things apart from the guards' weapons was the cutlery in front of the dinner guests.

150

She felt useless at the moment, apart from her ability to see when she was getting to Terrell.

"I'm certain that was a lie, Clarice, but as I'm sure you noticed, someone went to check just in case. You've at best bought yourself a couple of minutes. What do you think that will achieve?"

"Oh, I don't know, but every minute you're worried makes me *very happy*."

Clarice winked at him. It didn't come naturally to her, but she got the distinct sense it'd annoy him, and *that* certainly made her happier.

Chapter 35

Vincent was impressed at how Clarice handled herself. He'd always known she was tough, but seeing her egg Terrell on like that made him like her even more. She was clearly intentionally keeping their attention on her, and it must be in the hope that one of them would find a way to alter the odds.

His eyes moved from person to person in the room, making sure he knew exactly where everyone was.

Zo was right next to Terrell, with Rob on Terrell's other side, which made several guards focus on the two of them. That should make it easier for Jonas and him to act. Vincent mostly discounted the rest. They weren't bad in a fight, but they lacked the tactical instinct. He needed to make the first move and create enough trouble for the others to have a shot.

He figured he'd have a relatively decent chance of taking out the guard behind him without getting shot. The guard kept standing too close, and Vincent figured he'd be able to knock him out of position and disarm him.

But before acting, he was considering carefully what to do after that.

Terrell would probably grab Zo and have his guards converge on him and secure Clarice because he was now fixated on her. He'd probably be more concerned about getting to safety with a couple of them as hostages and calling reinforcements than trying to stand his ground.

To Vincent, that meant focusing on getting Terrell away from Zo in particular, and get a weapon to her.

He realized he'd basically have to concentrate on taking out the guards near a couple of crew members and assume they wouldn't get the idea of threatening to kill the rest quickly enough. He felt confident Terrell would be prepared to do that, which was another reason to get Zo a weapon as quickly as he could.

He looked over at Jonas and tried to signal, without drawing attention, that he would aim to take out the guard behind him. He hoped Jonas would understand and aim to do the same with his. Vincent nodded at the guards near Zo and Clarice. If Jonas understood and followed his lead, maybe they had a chance.

Vincent tensed up, getting ready to jump as soon as he noticed *his* guard getting too close again.

He sprang into action, grabbed the guard's plasma rifle and pushed it hard back at him. The guard instinctually fired and almost hit Rob across the table.

Vincent hit him in the face, and took advantage of holding on to the table while the guard had no firm support and threw the guard onto the table in front of him, using him as a shield.

"Stop him. Fire!"

Terrell attempted to go for Zo, just as Vincent expected. He was pleased to see Zo reacted almost as soon as he went for the guard. Before Terrell managed to do anything, Zo grabbed the knife from her plate and plunged it in his side.

Terrell howled in rage, as Vincent, with a firm grip of the plasma rifle of the guard he'd attacked, shot clean through the guard behind Zo.

Zo grabbed the capsule from where Terrell had stupidly left it on display as a trophy in front of where he'd sat and pushed herself away before Terrell managed to get himself together.

Next to Vincent, Jonas had knocked out his guard too and was using the guard as a shield while trying to fire at the guard behind Clarice.

Zo wrestled the rifle off the guard Vincent had shot and was crawling around the table. Vincent, Jonas, and Zo were all converging on the entrance where the prisoners had been brought in. The guards didn't seem very motivated to fight and ended up fleeing down the corridor.

Vincent looked for Terrell, and spotted him hiding behind a guard and Rob, who had a plasma rifle pointing at him.

"Give up, or your crewmate gets it."

Just as Terrell was finishing his sentence, the guard next to him slumped forward with a big hole straight through his chest. Vincent was covered in blood, with a look on his face that suggested he was in no mood to listen, and advanced on Terrell who bolted out the nearest entrance and sealed it without making good on his promise. They heard him yell for reinforcements.

"Everyone okay?"

153

They quickly confirmed everyone had gotten away without more than bruises and a couple of superficial burns. They got Clarice, Grant, and Mons out of their restraints. Grant seemed to be coming to, but was unsteady, and Vincent held him up. They grabbed the remaining plasma rifles off the guards they'd taken out.

"Clarice, best route to the ship? We need to get there fast and we need to expect to get shot at."

***

Clarice took the lead, and brought up the augmented map created from the public drawings, their scans, and what she'd compiled with her augmented eyes as she had been dragged to the observation deck. They were moving as fast as they could, bouncing on walls and the nominal floor like a pack of monkeys moving from tree to tree, jumping in long arcs due to the low gravity. At the first junction they got to, they ran into two bewildered guards that had clearly not been informed to expect an attack yet, and they were knocked out before they managed to lift their guns.

Near the halfway point, Clarice spotted what looked like an attempted ambush. Her eyes flagged up reflections in the side tunnels that suggested people waiting around the corner. They had no choice but to push past.

Clarice whispered to Vincent, and he took out the light. As they did, they could hear voices in the hallways. Clarice crept forward and fired at the first group and sent them bouncing down the tunnel.

The guards on the other side started firing toward her rifle blasts but she'd rolled away, and Vincent and Zo, who had their weapons trained on the tunnel already, fired rapidly after minor adjustments and took out at least two guards before the others retreated.

They fired a few more shots in both directions while they moved past and rushed further to avoid giving more of a chance.

"How do we get to the ship? They're bound to have guards there before us."

It was Vincent.

"Grant showed me a great trick earlier . . . You'll like it."

154

Clarice grinned.

"We'll get in and blow the windows in the docking area around the ship, or one of the other docking ports. They'll be forced to flee either into the ship or to the safety doors before they close."

"Lead on!"

Vincent seemed outright enthusiastic.

They shot at a few more guards on the way, but as expected, the main resistance came when they reached the docking area. More were probably on the way, followed by Terrell if he'd dare.

The guards were heavily armed and a couple of attempts at entering the area failed and they were forced to fall back.

They needed a clear ability to damage one of the docking ports enough to cause a breach, but they also needed to prevent getting stuck or overrun by desperate forces.

Jonas shot open several of the doors in the corridor they were in and everyone checked out the adjoining room looking for anything they might use. One was a storage room and Jonas rummaged through crates.

"Got chemical containers here . . ."

He had found several drums of flammable chemicals. Grant and Jonas got the containers ready and prepared fuses from strips of clothing dipped in one of the containers. They got as close as they could without getting shot at, lit a fuse, and sent the container spinning into the docking area, then repeated the process.

The guards in there shot at the first one and set off an explosion. They could hear yelling and people running.

After the third container, Vincent ran forward and shot at the lamps he could see, and Zo followed his lead. They didn't get all but darkened the docking area significantly.

Clarice pointed out guards for the rest while Grant and Jonas moved the last containers into place; hopefully to get a big enough explosion to crack the docking port adjoining the *Black Rain*.

They set it off with a plasma rifle, and within seconds they could feel the air pushed out through what started as a small crack that got bigger as the port gave in.

155

The guards that hadn't been sent packing by the burning chemical containers and the shooting were running towards the safety doors, while the crew ran for *Black Rain*.

The port was locked, but Clarice had bypassed the weak security of the docking ports once already and was able to open it in record time.

They got in and shut the doors just in time.

Everyone rushed toward the bridge to prepare for takeoff, grimly aware the station's weapons systems were bound to be charging, and even though they'd damaged the integrity of the docking area, the area they damaged earlier might have been fixed. In any case, Nautilus had one left and Terrell was bound to send ships after them.

Clarice scrambled for the comms console.

"Shit, Cap, comms is down."

"We'll deal with that later. For now, let's focus on getting away."

With everyone strapped in, Zo fired the navigation thrusters and started a crazy point turn inside the docking area. As soon as they were even roughly pointed toward the exit, she pushed the main engines to maximum, and everyone was pushed painfully hard back in their seats.

Near instantly they were hit by something, but nothing big enough to cause significant damage. So far.

"Status!"

Chapter 36

Terrell was furious. He bounced down the hallway from the observation deck, toward the bridge.

He called for reinforcements for the observation deck first and it took him a couple of valuable minutes before he realized what he needed to do was to stop them at the docks and slow them down before that to get more units in place.

He ordered a number of guards to try to intercept them, and all units near the docking ports to mass in front of *Black Rain*, but he knew they had enough of a head start that he could not get more than a quarter of his guards at most down there in time.

"Get me our cruisers, now! See who can get here soonest!"

He was yelling to his XO over the comms as he was entering the bridge where his XO was looking at security footage.

"They cannot get away. You understand? If they get away, someone will pay."

"Sir, the cruiser *Hammerhead* can be here in half an hour."

"Is that the closest?"

"Yes, sir . . . Sorry, sir."

Terrell threw a pen at the soldier in rage.

"How many do we have in the docking area?"

"Only fifteen men, sir," his XO replied. "Ten more are on the way. One unit tried ambushing them but had to retreat."

"Charge all weapons platforms. Now."

A young lieutenant relayed the orders to the staff manning the weapons consoles.

Terrell pulled up to him.

"If any ship leaves this station, I want it torn to pieces by our weapons. Understood? Any ship."

The XO brought the docking areas up on the screen. Seconds later it was lit up by burning canisters of something or other, and they could hear screaming over comms.

"Send people to the fighters in docking area three!" Terrell yelled to the first officer he could find.

"Those bastards are going to pull the same stunt as earlier and get away."

Just then, the alarms went off as the docking port next to *Black Rain* was burst open.

"Are you all amateurs? You caught them doing this shit hours ago, and you weren't prepared for them trying it again? Does nobody but me think around here?" The XO was shouting far louder than necessary, part out of anger and frustration, part because he was getting increasingly worried Terrell would turn on him if the situation didn't get under control quickly.

Terrell's face was contorted in a pained mix of rage and sheer hate.

"Launch the damn fighters. Get the damn cruiser to blow them up. Fire every weapon we have . . . I don't care what the hell you do."

"Just stop them, or we can't show our faces in Mars or Earth space again. Ever. Any of us. You understand?"

Terrell looked around the bridge.

"We're all fucked if you don't blow those shits up."

They could see *Black Rain* emerging at an angle out of the docking port and ramming the edge of it.

"NOW!"

Terrell was yelling as loud as he could, his voice breaking from the strain.

His weapons officers were desperately looking for a weapons lock. One of them got off a few shots and hit the ship once or twice, but didn't do much damage.

"I don't care if you have a lock. Launch everything. Litter space from here to the gate with explosives."

They started firing in the ship's general direction in a wide spread and launched what missiles they had.

Chapter 37

Black Rain narrowly evaded several missiles and quickly put enough distance between themselves and Nautilus that they had enough volume to navigate, so further missile attacks were pointless.

But Jonas picked up two fighter wings closing on them.

"Can we speed up any more? Fighters incoming."

"Engine is maxed, we're not going to outrun fighters that are mostly engine anyway," Clarice replied.

It was basics of fighting in space—it was all volume and mass ratio of engine and fuel to payload. To the extent a bigger ship could squeeze out a bit more efficiency they could have an upper hand, but a small, light fighter that was 80% engine and reaction-mass by mass, and maybe 50% by volume when pilot and weapons was accounted for would always be able to out-accelerate a ship like *Black Rain* that was carrying around a lot of extras.

Asking to try to outrun them was a dumb question, and Jonas realized this as soon as he'd asked.

He asked Grant for help manning the rear guns. Their advantage lay in more and mostly heavier munitions and better shielding. They didn't have any missiles or other particularly heavy-duty weaponry aboard—too hard to conceal when they wanted to fly to stations with more stringent security, but they did have a number of plasma guns powerful enough to blow these damn fighters up if they'd just manage to hit them.

Their biggest issue was that the fighters were small and had by far higher engine to payload proportions, which meant they could change direction much faster, but mostly there were *more* than them. They needed to desperately change that in their favor.

Since they had every reason to worry there'd be heavier ships coming, given the cruisers that attacked Vanguard, they couldn't afford to turn the ship around and coast, or rely on their navigation thrusters to keep accelerating, and so as long as the fighters were behind them, they'd be stuck with their smallest plasma guns.

"Make sure you're ready to switch to forward guns when they overtake us."

Jonas was certain they'd overtake and try to depend on rapid fly-bys and flipping to attack from multiple angles.

He relied on it—*Black Rain's* forward guns were much more powerful and had a wider angle of fire without being constrained by not hitting their own engines.

But he hoped they'd be able to take out a couple of fighters before that as well or at least spread the fighters out—every time they got shots close and forced one of the fighters to turn to avoid a shot, they'd lag behind the rest.

He was eager to prove to Vincent in particular that he could be as useful with the weapons as he could be in one-on-one combat.

"Focus on spreading them out. Fire at the ones further behind more."

Jonas was prepared to risk a few hits from the closest fighters if it meant they could increase the distance between them and allow them to focus on a smaller number at a time.

The first two fighters started firing at them. They were at the edge of their range still.

"Cap, be prepared, fighters incoming."

The captain altered the flight pattern to keep shifting direction just enough to make them a harder target, but the fighters would still have the advantage since they were a relatively speaking larger target.

"Grant, let's focus on the leaders; they're getting too close."

Jonas and Grant both swung their plasma guns toward the front fighters. Grant clipped one and damaged it enough that the pilot veered off on a wide arc.

The other passed them.

"Keep firing at the back, I'll take this one."

Jonas flipped to front weapons and took control of both stations with the help of their computerized targeting. He unleashed large volleys of plasma from all four of their forward guns in a spread that forced the fighter to desperately flip and try to head straight for them and get too close for him to aim.

160

Before he got that close, Jonas got in a shot directly through the cockpit and the engine at close range and the fighter exploded.

"Six more closing."

Grant was firing but, so far, they'd evaded all his shots

Jonas flipped back to take over one of the rear guns, and they tried to pincer another fighter, but with just two guns there were too many vectors for them to slip away.

A series of shots hit the ship from close enough that the ship shook.

"Damage report."

Mons reported minimal damage to one of their main engines, but otherwise nothing.

"Cap, we have to risk a flip, they're too close."

The captain nodded at Jonas.

"Okay. You heard him. Everyone ready. We're flipping the ship."

They cut the main engine and instantly fired navigation thrusters to rotate the ship 180 degrees, putting the forward guns facing the fighters. As the engines cut, they were effectively weightless except for the minor effect of the flip, which was a nice temporary relief from the heavy g of the acceleration.

As soon as they hit 90, Grant and Jonas were able to start targeting the lead fighters, and they got the first in a pincer and destroyed it within seconds.

The others scattered and tried shooting, but while Grant and Jonas worked the targeting systems, the rest worked to keep rotating the ship and predicting angles to keep the front aimed to maximize the potential targets. It was disorienting, but the computer systems steadied Grant and Jonas' views enough that they could keep focus.

The fighters separated and tried approaching from different directions. As soon as they realized what was happening, Jonas asked for main engine thrust and the two approaching from the front suddenly found *Black Rain* hurtling towards them, accelerating as hard as they could. They tried to take evasive action, but when they did, they both flew straight into the field of the forward plasma guns.

As soon as they were out, they flipped the ship again, fired the main thrusters to let the fighters coming from behind approach, then flipped 90 degrees sideways so they could fire all forward guns right as one of the fighters trying to evade them flew past.

The two remaining fighters got in a couple of hits that did minor damage, but these pilots appeared to be pretty green, Jonas thought.

"Let's try to make them dance . . ."

Zo and Grant both knew what he meant, and they turned the ship toward the two last fighters, and accelerated towards them.

Jonas and Grant focused on one fighter each, firing ahead of them with each set of forward guns, forcing them to keep changing direction, and moving them closer and closer to each other.

Once the pilots realized what was going on, and that they were being herded toward each other, it seemed like they realized their only option was to try to turn—the greater distance they put between themselves and the *Black Rain*, the broader the dispersal of the plasma fire would be.

But *Black Rain* was accelerating as hard as she could, and as the fighters turned and focused on running instead of evading, they made easier targets.

As soon as he saw the light of their rear engines on the main screen, Jonas knew they had them, and within a few seconds, they disappeared from the screen in a flash of light.

The crew didn't cheer. They quietly got the ship back en route to the Mars-Earth gate.

Once they were again on the optimal course, they accelerated as hard as they could, which meant they'd have to wait to assess damage until later, as the g-force would make it too hazardous to get around the ship.

Chapter 38

"I think we're clear."

Clarice kept a close eye on the scanners for any signs of additional fighters, but they were all gone. There was still the question if any larger, faster ships were closing in on them or not, but for the moment, they appeared to be okay.

It gave them a moment to assess the situation. Clarice's first thought was to see if they could get the clips they had collected on Nautilus out.

The comms array appeared to be offline. It could potentially be damaged from the fight. She started running diagnostics.

Nothing appeared.

"Captain, I can't get comms online."

Zo turned and nodded.

"Any idea why?"

"Not yet, Cap, running diagnostics."

"The latest broadcasts we got were shortly after arriving at Nautilus. Either they jammed us or something happened then. Could still be a combination of jammers and damage, or something else."

The diagnostics didn't reveal any obvious damage from their battle with the fighters. They'd need to get someone outside to rule out everything, but that was not an option while accelerating hard.

She started a second set of internal diagnostics to try to see if she could pinpoint any issues in the comms system itself.

"In the meantime, these are the last broadcasts we got . . . Some interesting bits in there . . ."

***

Clarice put the broadcast on the main shared view. There were two high-priority items.

First was a general notification of heightened security in Mars and Earth space with an attached statement from the Cabinet press office accusing *forces within the Mars Colony* of sedition and standing behind terrorists accused of carrying out the Vanguard attack.

The statement was brief and non-committal, but it did contain a warning at the end that the government wouldn't tolerate such attacks and was committed to the integrity of the system-wide union and would defend it at all costs.

It was a pretty clear threat of reprisals.

The second statement had more direct relevance to them. It was a request for information about the ship *Black Rain* and its crew. It wasn't an arrest warrant. They were wanted for questioning as witnesses to the Vanguard attack.

Of course, Clarice thought to herself, chances were significant they had her face on file, and odds were high they had correlated it with security footage of them that could be tied back to the ship, so she wasn't sure the distinction between an arrest warrant and wanting them for questioning really mattered.

It meant they'd be treated nicer if identified, perhaps.

Clarice exchanged glances with Zo. She knew the captain would understand the considerations and would be as disinclined as she was to trust they'd be safe with Earth authorities. On the other hand, Earth seemed like it might be the less trigger-happy of the parties involved, and so, if they couldn't get evidence against Terrell out, surrendering to Earth authorities might be the safest option.

***

Clarice's scans came back inconclusive. Something was up with the internals of the comms system. Something might also be up due to the fighters, but without fixing the internal issue, she wouldn't know. She couldn't open the console and get to the relevant components as long as they were accelerating hard.

They were still receiving some signals, but seemed entirely unable to transmit, which also meant their comms system was unable to request retransmit when there were errors in inbound data, so they only got best-effort, initial broadcast signals.

She was reminded of her moment of surprise when Mons appeared to have caught Grant out while doing searches to the comms console. She couldn't really believe Grant would have done something. Why would he? He had no motive she was aware of for doing anything.

All he'd done that she could see were searches anyway.

She opened a private text-only channel to the captain.

Cap. 'Something' wrong with internals of comm system. Need to open it up when acc. burn over. Don't understand why. Grant tripped a security check at comms console on Nautilus . . .

She looked over at Zo, and could see from her face she'd read the message.

Must be something else. No way he'd do something like that.

Clarice was inclined to agree. She didn't want to believe it either. And something about Mons' reaction troubled her. Maybe he had done something and was worried Grant would notice. She was a lot more inclined to think Mons could be capable of something.

Let's see what I find when I open it up . . . With this right after the gas and Terrell's lies . . .

We'll talk later. Don't mention comms issue to anyone else until we know more. No need to worry everyone.

Clarice kept probing the system, trying to narrow the problem down as much as she could so she'd be able to get right to it when she could get out of her seat. She hated having to deal with hardware. So messy and unpredictable compared to software. But she hated being trussed up in her seat, unable to get out to diagnose the hardware even more.

These damn long, hard acceleration burns were always irritating. It was always when you were unable to stand up and the bridge gimbal was unlocked to deal with the chance of rapid course changes so you couldn't safely even exit the bridge that you suddenly had all kinds of reasons to want to get up and walk around.

They could lock the bridge in position now, she supposed—they were accelerating for the gate only. But the captain wanted to be ready in case they were surprised by any more forces.

"Something on the scanners," Jonas yelled just as she thought about it.

"It's coming from the direction of Nautilus."

Clarice checked the scanners.

"Looks like it's a ship incoming. Still far away, but it appears to be gaining on us."

This was no fighter. The mass was several times theirs, at least. What little they could tell seemed to fit the media descriptions of the cruisers that attacked Vanguard.

"Record everything. If these are the ones that attacked Vanguard, and they start shooting at us, we want evidence we're not on their side . . ."

For the time being, there was little they could do. Their engine output was at max.

Clarice ran some numbers.

"Captain, we should still have some distance when we reach the gate, but if we assume standard weapons, we'll be in weapons range for a few minutes. If they time it right, they have time for a couple of missile barrages and throwing wide range plasma fire at us."

They could hope the ship following them would be challenged by Hercules or Deimos stations and that this would buy them enough time.

Chapter 39

Zo was worried about the ship approaching from Nautilus, but she felt certain there would be enough of a military presence near the gate to deter their attackers. Her biggest concern was their lack of ability to get a comms link, but they could not take the risk of stopping their acceleration burn until they were closer to the gate, and with the engines on, trying to fix the system was not going to go well.

"Unidentified ship, this is Deimos Guardian. You are coming in too hot into a restricted zone. You're ordered to slow down and surrender to inspection."

The message was repeated two more times. Their inbound feed was relatively reliable this close to the big relays, but without the ability to transmit, their best hope was that Deimos would either believe they'd not heard the message or at least be careful about making assumptions.

Just a bit closer, and they should see the ship following them.

Of course, Zo realized, there was the risk they'd see the ship following and assume they were part of an attack, even though it didn't make tactical sense to attack this spread out.

"Unidentified ship, you are ordered to stand down."

"Weapons lock, Captain. Looks like they're aiming almost everything at us.

"We're also detecting at least three destroyers ahead."

"Clarice, time to try to fix that comm system." Zo looked briefly over at her.

"Shut down the main engine, but don't brake just yet. They won't shoot when we've made a sign we're complying."

Zo wasn't sure that was true, but they'd far overshoot the gate even if they flipped and braked as hard as they could anyway. They'd been accelerating at max speed for several hours, so it'd take several hours to stop.

As soon as they shut down the engine and were finally free of the g-forces, Clarice unbuckled and started opening the comms panel to look for the problem.

167

"Unidentified ship, we require you to start braking, not just cutting your engine. This is your last warning."

"Cap, a suggestion. Let's try to send a message with our navigation thrusters while we start the brake."

Vincent looked at her. She nodded at him. It was worth a try. Certainly better than nothing.

"Clarice, we're re-engaging thrusters. Back in your seat."

She flipped the ship and re-engaged the main thrusters.

"All yours, Vincent. Be brief and make sure to get their attention first."

Vincent started pulsing their rear navigation thruster, causing slight jerks, but the navigation thruster's output was less than ten percent of the main thruster. He sent SOS several times, and they waited for a sign from Deimos it was enough.

"Unidentified ship, SOS received. We're assuming you have comms trouble, not clear what other problems. Elaborate using same method."

Zo felt some tension dissipate—at least they had a way to get messages through.

The ship following them was getting closer, though, and as their speed was dropping, it would have them in weapons range sooner than expected.

Vincent pulsed the navigation thruster more. He started by transmitting their ship id. The genuine one.

"Followed by hostile ship. Request assistance. Important data on Vanguard attack onboard."

Zo hoped they'd believe them, at least enough to not shoot them down. Deimos was under Mars control. If anybody wanted to know who was really behind the Vanguard attack, it would be them.

"*Black Rain*, you are wanted for questioning. Continue braking, we have the ship following you on scanners and will deal with them."

Their sensors showed one of the Earth destroyers ahead starting to accelerate toward them, but on a course that would overshoot. Hopefully, they were preparing to make their follower stand down.

They kept braking as hard as they could. Deimos requested course corrections that seemed like the first step of a maneuver to get them to bleed speed while keeping them as close as practical. It wouldn't save much.

168

They were just a couple of minutes away from being in weapons range of the ship following them when the Earth destroyer passed by.

Suddenly two more Earth destroyers gated in.

One of them immediately targeted Deimos Guardian. The other locked their weapons on *Black Rain*.

"What the hell is going on?"

"*Black Rain*, this is Earth destroyer *Ariane*. You are to surrender to Hercules Station immediately. We have been briefed about your communications problems. You will align your engines as follows, and acknowledge understanding using your navigation thrusters as previously done. Failure to comply will mean destruction."

That explained the weapons lock on Deimos. Earth was not prepared to let the Mars government get their hands on them first.

However, it also made Zo worry whether they could be sure that they'd make it to Hercules, or whether some of the people involved might be in Terrell's pockets.

Weapons fire was detected and she brought the data up on her console. The ship following them had engaged the first Earth destroyer in battle. Their follower fired first, and appeared to have hit the destroyer's main weapons array before the Earth ship had even been ready to fire. The second salvo took out their engines. The ship was no longer a threat but their follower cleaved it with a powerful plasma cannon anyway.

Zo made her mind up. Whether or not *Ariane* was bought or Hercules command was safe, she couldn't trust that they'd succeed in defending them. Their speed was too high to be able to get close enough for Deimos Guardian to protect them.

"Everyone, we're going through that gate. No matter what. Any objections?"

Nobody objected.

"Clarice, do your magic and make it look like we're losing control. Then shortest curve towards the Mars-belt gate instead of the Earth gate that leaves the Earth ships between us and Terrell's people if we can."

169

The belt gate wasn't much further, and given the course change Deimos Guardian had put them on, it was actually going to be significantly easier to get to.

The ship soon started spinning wildly; the unpredictable turns happened too quickly for the bridge gimbal to keep the perceived gravity in a single direction, and Zo got nauseated. From the faces of her crew, the same applied to most of them. Except for Jonas, who seemed to be able to take all of it with ease.

Zo had both Deimos Guardian and *Ariane* shouting in her ear.

She ignored them. Soon the ship started shooting on an arc toward the gate. They had little maneuverability, and they just had to hope everyone would be too busy to consider shooting at them.

Deimos and *Ariane* kept shouting for them to stop. *Ariane* put weapons lock at them just as their followers took out a second Earth destroyer. Shortly afterward, they could see *Ariane* break off what had started as a pursuit of them and turn towards their followers.

Deimos also dropped their targeting and started firing at the ship following them.

Finally. Everyone realized who the actual threat is, Zo thought to herself.

They were approaching the gate at a far higher speed than they should be, but Zo knew the safety margins allowed for it.

She asked Jonas and Grant to keep the weapons stations manned, in case they still had to look out.

Their follower seemed to be trying to evade the Earth destroyer and cut towards them. While doing so, they managed to get *Ariane* in between themselves and Deimos, and the station was forced to stop firing.

"Cap, we have incoming."

Jonas had detected a huge barrage of missiles. He and Grant took out two almost immediately.

Ariane started firing at the missile barrage too and took out three more. There were still five incoming when *Ariane* had to focus on a missile barrage heading straight for them instead.

"*Ariane's* engines are down . . . They're still firing."

"Holy . . . Captain, they're accelerating straight for our attacker."

170

Zo watched on screen as *Ariane* clipped their attacking ship and damaged their engines before breaking up.

"*Black Rain* . . . This is *Ariane*. Run! Our core is about to blow. We can't help you further, but given our shared opponent is attacking us to get you, I feel inclined to trust we are on the same side. All we can do is broadcast our data of this encounter to Earth. *Ariane*, out."

Jonas got another missile, but Zo was focused on the images of *Ariane* breaking apart, and exploding, and of their attacker continuing to limp towards them.

A few escape pods looked like they'd made it off as *Ariane* blew, but by no means all.

Another Earth destroyer gated in, but it was too far away. They'd either make it to the belt gate or be destroyed long before it could do anything. Besides, given what their attacker had done to the destroyers so far, it might not matter.

Grant cheered as he took out another missile, but overall the bridge was subdued.

With *Ariane* out of the way, Deimos was able to re-target their attacker and fired what they had, but that too would be too late.

They were just seconds away from triggering the gate when one of the missiles hit the side of the ship, and nearly every alarm on Zo's panel went red.

Chapter 40

"All stations. Status!" Zo could see the same status displays as everyone else, but she wanted everyone to dig into the details and digest anything vital.

The ship was severely damaged, but at least one of the main engines was still working, and no atmosphere was venting.

She decided to take the risk of sustaining maximum burn for the next few minutes to accelerate them away at a decent rate before starting repairs. They aimed at an asteroid that was within a few hours with the planned burn.

As soon as the main engine went off, the ship was dark to the outside, given their radio transponders were off. It should make them hard enough to notice—they'd not detected any nearby ships when they passed through the gate.

That, in itself, was somewhat worrying given recent events.

The crew started going over the ship to carry out repairs, and Clarice was finally able to investigate the comms problem.

Overall, they were in better shape than Zo had feared. They quickly did another few minutes' burn after giving everyone enough warning to strap in, and cut an hour off their path to the asteroid. Soon, they started brief retro burns with their nav thrusters to swing around it.

It was a tiny asteroid, but enough to put between them and the gate to make them functionally invisible for anyone following.

Vincent worked on issues with three of the plasma guns and reported he was confident they'd be in order within a few hours.

Otherwise, there were a few holes in the outer bulkhead that had automatically been sealed with the injection of a cement-like substance that hardened in seconds. It was more brittle than a proper fix, and they'd want it looked at when they could get to a proper dock, but it'd hold for now.

"Captain, I've found the comm problem."

Clarice was wielding a circuit board that was totally burnt out.

"We have two problems. First is that this burned out. The second is that we have no spare. I know for a fact we had spares two weeks ago, and we've not used them."

172

"It sounds like you're suggesting sabotage."

"I don't see any other option. I double-checked inventory. It was there. I put it there. My record was counter-signed by Mons. I've asked him, he swears it was there."

"You know that thing I mentioned to you. We need to talk to Grant. Find out what he was doing."

Clarice looked at Zo with pursed lips and what Zo could swear was a red glow in her eyes.

"Couldn't it just as well have been the search party at Nautilus?"

"I thought about that. But the damage requires familiarity with our comms system. Our system is not standard issue. It's an old model that's been modified several times. To know burning out this card would make a difference is one thing, they could have just gotten lucky, but to know what to damage and to know to remove our spares is another. It could be Grant, but the more I think about it, the more I think it must be Mons. He knew about the spares. And he looked worried when Grant poked around the comms console."

Zo looked at Clarice and nodded. She thought Mons was the more likely suspect, too. But they had to talk to Grant at least.

"We will talk to Grant. But not yet. Let's get to a station first. If we start talking to people about this, and we're wrong about Mons, I don't want to risk alerting whomever did this while we're vulnerable."

The glow in Clarice's eyes was gone, as was the tension in her neck. Zo knew her well enough to know Clarice would see the sense in what she had said.

"Let's keep this between us, Clarice. I promise we'll find out what happened. In the meantime, let's see if you can figure out a workaround."

"I'm not sure it's possible to work around it, Cap. We don't have many components onboard, but I'll try. Watch your back, okay?"

"You too." Zo smiled at her and Clarice smiled back.

Zo wasn't sure how to feel about her. She felt impossible to read at times—sometimes relentless and confident, other times so guarded and awkward.

Chapter 41

Jonas finished helping Vincent with repairs to the last of the plasma guns and made his way down toward the engine room to help Grant out with the second engine.

The two had never really hit it off, but they worked well enough together. Grant felt too serious to Jonas. He seemed constantly focused on going about work in a dour way that Jonas found quite annoying. Jonas was in space because it was an adventure to him. An escape from an earth he saw as boring and stagnating.

Grant, on the other hand, from what he'd told Jonas anyway, had seen space as a place for grueling work mining asteroids out in the belt. Physically demanding work had left him muscular, and of a similarly big build to Vincent already before that; well, probably with several scars. But it was also psychologically demanding—the mining treks often involved slow, lengthy journeys with minimal crew that often hardly saw each other as they put boosters on small asteroids and constantly adjusted equipment while they got them close enough to a gate within the smallest fuel expense possible.

When Jonas got to the engine room, it seemed Grant was still struggling to find the problems with the engine. The casings for several modules were strapped to the floor in case they had to accelerate. Parts neatly placed in boxes, while Grant was swearing at something or other.

"Anything I can help with?"

Grant turned to look at him.

"I don't know . . . How well do you know our engines?"

"Not very well. I know the design in theory, but I've not taken them apart quite like this."

Jonas motioned to all the parts spread out.

"It's okay. I think I know which components have burned out, but we need to get several more parts out to get to them. Whoever designed this piece of shit should be hung behind a mining transport during acceleration . . ."

Jonas hadn't often seen Grant smile, and seeing him smile now was unsettling. Grant turned back to the part he was trying to pull out, and Jonas moved to give him a hand.

"So what do you think? Will the Sovereign Earth people come after us out here?"

"They kinda have to, don't they? We broke their trust, and now we're about to turn them in."

Grant looked unhappy.

"They lied to us. And their mission was fake."

"I'm sure they had their reasons," Grant followed up. "That gate . . . It can't be good. I mean, why did they just give it all to us?"

Jonas had some sympathy for that argument too. Like a lot of people, he wanted to see what was on the other side—it was what had made him find work in space after all, but it scared him too. Like Zo, he'd been shocked when he heard the claims the job was based on, but felt betrayed when finding out it was all lies.

"Too late now anyway . . . They'll kill us if they get a chance, we know too much." Jonas was a pragmatist, and whatever he might think about what Grant said, immediate survival mattered more.

"Maybe if we offered to stay quiet about the missions . . . If you think about it, they just didn't tell us everything—everything else was our own fault. We were sneaking around. And we ran off. Doesn't feel right."

Grant kept his eyes on the engine components he was lifting out and labeling while he was talking.

Jonas didn't know what to make of what he'd said, and they kept working quietly. Fifteen minutes later they'd replaced a couple of burned-out parts and re-assembled the engine.

"Cap, we're ready for an engine test. Just give us a minute to clear the room."

They pulled themselves out into the hallway and sealed the room in case anything went wrong, then signaled to the bridge.

The test went okay. They checked the sensors in the engine room and no overheating or radiation.

"We're okay, Cap. Heading to the bridge now."

175

With the engine and weapons fixed, most of the other repairs could wait. Jonas and Grant pulled their way along the hallway to the bridge and strapped in.

Everyone else was there already, waiting.

***

Zo had picked a small trading outpost a couple of travel away. It'd take half a day of hard acceleration followed by several annoying course changes to avoid asteroids in the way, then a hard deceleration burn. It was far enough, she hoped, that they'd have at least some warning if anyone were to follow, and far enough they were unlikely to run into military ships. They'd be vulnerable to being spotted by followers for the first burn, so she'd adjusted the headings on purpose so it looked like they'd be aiming for a larger trading station further out in the belt.

Assuming they saw no ships on sensors, they'd make their first navigation adjustment to get behind an asteroid relative to the gate and their path, and then turn further and do another brief pulse of their main engines to alter their path enough to slip far enough away before their next round of navigation changes.

The long deceleration burn would happen with the ship turned around, their dark side—and main weapons—facing any followers.

It still worried Zo massively that Clarice had made no advances on rigging up an alternative comms system, even with Vincent helping out. She'd given Mons other tasks on purpose, in case Clarice's suspicions were right.

When they were within an hour or so of the trading outpost, they might be able to get a radio signal through. If not, they'd repeat their nav-thruster morse trick to explain to C&C on the station.

That wasn't her concern.

The concern was that as long as they were unable to send copies of their data to someone to broadcast, Terrell, and who knew how many Sovereign Earth ships, might be after them, and see destroying them as sufficient to prevent the spread of the information. And they didn't know if they could trust anyone else either.

Then there was Clarice's suspicion of sabotage. Zo couldn't quite believe it, but she did believe Clarice was just as thorough as she insisted she'd been, and if she said there was no other option, then it needed to be taken seriously.

She badly wanted to investigate right now. But right now they were desperately vulnerable. Still lots of damage they'd not fixed. No comms. As long as their main engines were burning and they were all on the bridge, if anyone had sabotaged anything, they wouldn't be in a position to try anything.

If Clarice was right, she had to assume it'd come to a head once they got to the station ahead. Zo was certain she could depend on Clarice, but who else was absolutely above suspicion?

Vincent and Jonas seemed obvious. Clarice seemed to suspect Mons, and Zo had to admit it was a possibility. But he'd always struck Zo as obedient to the point of submission and didn't seem the type. That left Rob and Grant. Rob didn't seem like he'd have the knowledge or inclination. Grant, well Zo didn't think Grant would have enough initiative, and besides, what would he gain from it?

Motive struck Zo as the biggest problem. Could any of them have motive? Unless they'd bought Terrell's lies like she had . . .

But they had all seen the same clips she had of Terrell conspiring to lie.

Chapter 42

A sudden alarm flagged up on all of the bridge screens. They were due for one of their navigation burns to get in position to decelerate, but their scanners had just picked up a major ship heading in the direction they'd initially been flying.

Someone had clearly picked up their burn, and someone had gotten hold of the vector.

They couldn't pick up any transponder signals. To Zo, that meant they were almost inevitably from Nautilus. Earth or Mars military wouldn't hide like that, and the ship was too big to expect pirates.

At the moment, they were shielded enough by nearby asteroids that they'd not show up on any radar scans, and fortunately, they picked up on the ship before firing their navigation thrusters, so the ship wouldn't have recognized up any drive signatures.

Problem was what would happen when they got closer. At their acceleration, they might be able to pick up the *Black Rain* on scans within the next hour. They wouldn't be close enough to be able to say for sure if she was an asteroid or a ship, but that'd only be true if they remained dark, and thus defenseless.

The moment they fired up a main engine, a nav thruster, or weapons, they'd light up on that ship's screen. Even their active scans would soon be too noisy, in spite of the randomization applied to them, Zo realized.

"Turn those scans off. NOW."

And so, they were blind.

"Any ideas? We can't sit here. If they've followed us, they'll certainly scan for any object that appears to possibly have come from the path they're taking. Even some simple scans and they'll see a single object flying away from their path without spin or anything."

"We might not need the thrusters to fix that."

Vincent had a smug grin on his face.

"I've not done it with a ship this big before . . ."

"*What* is it you haven't done, Vincent?"

It wasn't like him not to get straight to the point.

"Basic thermodynamics, Captain. The specifics are not my strength, but the nav thrusters simply work by ejecting energetic particles, right? The thrust is proportional to the energy we eject."

Zo nodded. "Your point, Vincent?"

"They can detect our nav thrusters because they're hot. Highly excited matter, ejected at high speed. They can't detect if we throw a bunch of mass overboard. Even with an active scan it just looks like any other mass unless it's something exotic and concentrated.

"Our water tanks are nearly full. We haven't traveled much, and our current speed is low. If we dump most of our water as a jet, we might get enough thrust to adjust our course enough to look like we're coming from another direction. We can send ourselves into a slow, unstable spin that will look plausible for an asteroid but not for a ship."

Zo lightened up. Vincent's idea didn't sound entirely crazy. She wasn't sure they'd get enough thrust, but it was worth running the numbers.

"The final piece, Cap, is that we empty most of the rest of our water, including our waste water, in every direction. It will diffuse their scans enough that we'll look uneven enough to look less like a ship. We did this once . . . On a mission."

He trailed off. Zo knew he didn't like talking about his military missions. He'd survived most of the people in his unit before he left. The few stories he'd told her almost invariably involved the death of one or more people he'd known personally.

"Let's run the numbers, people. Clarice, you lead. Simulate the possible trajectories with Vincent. Get us something believable."

It was potentially a huge gamble. Get it wrong and they'd just draw more attention to themselves. But Zo couldn't think of any other options, and nobody else had offered up anything.

Their speed was high enough she worried they'd be unable to alter direction enough to not be suspicious. Though, if they were lucky and could get the right trajectory to look plausibly natural, a spin that didn't make sense for a ship might just confuse their followers long enough.

179

They still needed to be able to adjust their course to get to their target without being noticed, though. They wouldn't be able to do that unless their followers put considerable distance between them. Along their opponent's present trajectory, it wouldn't take long before they'd be in a relative direction where the *Black Rain* would be unable to do the right deceleration burn without the plume being detectable to them at great distance.

Worst case it meant a lengthy detour.

Zo was still lost in thought when Clarice and Vincent moved next to her.

"You're not going to like this, Cap, but we've found a way to make Vincent's idea work."

"What am I not going to like about it?"

"There's a small asteroid ahead. Our scans before we went dark shows it's low density. Mostly rubble. Some water ice. If we eject water at the right time, we can crash into it."

"You were right. I don't like it. What's your projected effect?"

"We should incur minimal damage. We think both our ship and a pile of rubble ought to break off in similar directions, along with a minor course change for the rest of the asteroid. A scan afterwards should show a relatively normal minor collision, but they shouldn't be able to reliably tell the original directions as they won't know which bits broke off from what or due to what kind of energetic event and how it affected the course of the relevant bodies. Especially not if we dump the rest of our water around the time of the impact.

"And our post-impact speed and direction should be reduced enough to make us less conspicuous."

The captain certainly did not like the idea, but she trusted both Clarice and Vincent a great deal.

"Triple check everything. Get Grant to check it too; if there's one thing he knows, it's the effects of impacts. I'm not going to crash the ship on purpose without you being damn sure everything checks out."

"I'd just like to remind you that Clarice has successfully crashed this ship before," Vincent added with a broad grin.

As Clarice and Vincent pushed over to Grant to discuss the numbers, she motioned for Jonas, relayed the plan, and asked him to check all systems to see if any other preparations needed to be made if they went along with it.

180

It didn't take long for Grant to confirm Clarice's calculations, and they set to work to prepare, while they were effectively in the dark, unable to detect anything but what they passively received out of fear of giving away their position.

Grant, Vincent, and Jonas went to prepare the water systems. The tanks were connected to ports on the ship exterior, and luckily, the ship's orientation would allow them to eject the water in the right direction by attaching only a very minimal piece of pipe to direct the flow.

The only positive being that they detected no scans from the other ship. All they picked up was the radiation from their engine plume that confirmed they were still on the same heading.

It felt like they'd been waiting for hours when Vincent contacted them from just inside the airlock.

"We're ready. On your command."

"Everyone strap in."

Zo looked around the bridge, and waited for everyone to be back in their positions, and got confirmation from Vincent that they were strapped in too. They'd stay by the airlock in case adjustments would be needed.

"Go ahead."

The shift was minor at first. The perceived gravity from the jet was tiny. It'd shift their direction only a few degrees. They let out a small burst first and turned on a narrow external scanning beam facing the asteroid they wanted to crash with. They were turning, but it would be closer than hoped.

Zo ordered a longer burst, and bit by bit they aligned their heading with the small low-density asteroid.

"Shit. Cap, one of the tank valves appears to have jammed."

They were close, but at their current heading, they'd plow almost straight into the asteroid instead of grazing it.

They tried another burst, but the jammed valve on one of the tanks cut their performance significantly.

"Clarice, adjust calculations. What will be the effect if we lose that trust?"

"Vincent, do what you can to try to fix it . . ."

Zo looked expectantly at Clarice, whose eyes had blacked out while she was focusing on the calculations. Without re-enabling her normal sight, she relayed her findings.

The numbers weren't too bad. They'd risk more damage, but their course adjustment would still be okay.

"No luck, Cap; the valve is stuck. We can go outside and try to force it open manually . . ."

"Too risky. Stand down. Prepare for impact—we've got about ten minutes. Secure the airlock."

"We better hope that asteroid is as low density as we think . . ."

The captain was speaking to nobody in particular. There was nothing they could do, but wait as the ship was coasting, mostly blind and deaf, with no acceleration to give them a feeling of motion.

It felt as if their breathing collectively slowed and stopped as they anticipated the crash. The minutes stretched out. An occasional beep from a monitor signaling passive scans had detected nothing of consequence.

Then they felt the crash.

Chapter 43

The ship decelerated suddenly and quite hard, but within tolerance levels. Clarice glanced on her sensors and it registered equivalent to 4g. That should be well within what the ship could handle, depending on whether any particularly sensitive areas were hit harder than the rest.

The sound was eerie; the vibrations of the impact with the outer bulkhead, muted by the inner layers. Alarms went off for a few minor leaks, sealed automatically by expanding foam.

Then there was the sound of metal under stress shifting and bending. The sound was almost that of someone crying. Piercing at first, the pitch dropping as the vibrations dampened. Slowly becoming a deep bass; a growl.

The volume dropped, and so did the g-force. They'd pushed through the densest part of the asteroid, and lost most of their speed from hitting the rubble, which mercifully had been no worse than they'd expected. They appeared to have created a hole straight through, but pushing enough material in front of them and to the side that the hole was creating a cone widening to the point where the asteroid was starting to break apart.

They dared switch on some low-powered scans, and confirmed a significant chunk had been jettisoned, and their own speed and course had been significantly altered.

As they exited, Vincent sent a message that he'd blow a vent to ditch most of the rest of their water if the captain approved it. She did, and the last burst of water sent them into a slow spin.

They'd not be able to reasonably navigate like this, but that wasn't the point. If the ship following them spotted them at a distance now, it'd be highly unlikely they'd believe they were, in fact, a ship.

Still, they waited. Their passive scan continues to pick up faint radiation from the other ship's drive. They were still on the same course.

Then, there was a ping. A trace of an active scan. They picked up a series of pulses suggesting a wide, relatively low power scan from a significant distance.

As far as Clarice could tell, there'd be no chance they'd see more than a blob of mass wobbling in line with their rotation, and with a path that fit an intersection with several asteroid fragments. Nothing ought to cause suspicion.

Yet the ship lingered. A number of additional scans followed over the next half an hour. Hour . . .

Hours later, the scans appeared to end, and their own passive receivers suggested the ship might be turning. They'd have to wait maybe another twelve hours before they could be sure they were gone or far enough away to restart their own engines and limp to the station they were aiming for.

Clarice and the captain were relieved by Jonas and Rob. They'd been at it about as long, but Clarice didn't object. She headed for her cabin. It felt like the first opportunity to rest since this whole thing started.

And who knew what would happen once they made it to the station. They still needed to get a message out and get to safety afterwards.

Zo was right in front of her and they reached her cabin first.

"Hey, Clarice, want to come in for a drink?"

Clarice only hesitated for a second.

"Sure."

She looked at Zo and followed her into her cabin. She looked exhausted. Her hair streaked and frizzled. Her eyelids heavy. She was still pretty. She always struck Clarice as though she looked like she could take on anything . . . Clarice knew the story of how she'd gotten her command, and it was one of the reasons why she was on the crew. The loyalty and sense of family mattered to her.

Zo handed her a covered cup and decanted scotch into it.

"Need any water with that?"

"Neat is fine."

Clarice didn't know why she said that. She hardly ever drank, and certainly not neat scotch. She sipped the drink while Zo downed hers in one go, to the extent you could *down* something from a cup that looked like a children's sippy-cup suitable for zero-g.

184

The captain's cabin was just as small as hers. Now, in practically zero-g, it didn't really matter—every surface was usable. Still, they were close together.

Zo was looking at her, quietly observing her face. Normally, Clarice would have no problems keeping eye contact without blinking. She could turn down the intensity at will and stare back at someone however long she wanted.

But somehow, the captain's piercing look intimidated her and excited her at the same time.

Clarice knew the captain found her attractive. Or thought she knew anyway. She didn't know for a fact if Zo liked women. She wasn't sure if she did. But she was drawn to Zo in any case.

Zo moved closer and touched her hair.

"We haven't spent much time together."

She smiled, but Clarice thought there was a tinge of sadness to her smile.

"You've been very impressive, Clarice."

Zo's voice deepened and slowed, before she suddenly pulled back a bit and laughed.

"Don't worry, I'm not going to seduce you tonight. Maybe some other night."

She gave Clarice an exaggerated wink, and Clarice was sure she must be going red, and looked down. She was not used to feeling so off-kilter—usually she was the one intimidating people. Men twice her age reduced to stuttering fools.

"I just wanted some company for a bit tonight. This shit has me on edge."

Clarice relaxed a bit, though she was looking at the captain in a different way.

"We'll be okay, Cap. Once we get the data out, they'll have no reason to risk anything to get to us."

"I hope you're right. Fuck. I shouldn't have taken this damn job."

"We all agreed, Cap."

"In here, you call me Zara. And thanks for saying that."

Clarice blushed again and motioned towards the door.

"I should go."

185

"Scaring you again, *huh?*" Zara smiled. "Sure. We both need sleep," she added.

She pushed herself over to Clarice and brushed against her.

"I'm sure we'll have occasion for another drink soon . . ."

Clarice slid into the hallway.

"Good night . . . Zara."

She barely whispered the name as Zara slid the door shut. Clarice's pulse was racing as she pulled herself down to her cabin and entered. She cleaned up and strapped into her bunk, but she couldn't get Zo, Zara out of her head, and it took her longer to fall asleep than usual.

Chapter 44

"Morning, Grant."

Grant looked startled.

Morning was arbitrary given they had no source of *truth*. They were on UTC because they'd not had a reason to adjust lately—Vanguard was on UTC. And Rob didn't even know what Nautilus was on, but odds were UTC. Most stations were. Made life simpler when you didn't have to deal with planetary time zones to stick to whatever most others used.

So it was morning for them after their first calm night in several days.

"Anything I can help you with?"

Rob had nothing to do in the medical bay at the moment, and so had volunteered to help Vincent carry out maintenance. The storage bay had survived with just minor damage from a couple of containers that had been dislodged and bounced off the walls.

"Morning . . . Didn't expect to see you here. Just getting some tools."

Grant slid over to a tool cabinet, and Rob turned back to what he was doing.

"So, crazy few days, *huh*?"

This was Rob's first time on a job that involved this level of physical struggle, and it had rattled him severely.

He turned toward Grant, happy to have someone to talk to.

"Yeah, I guess."

"What are you looking for there? There are no tools in the safe."

Grant looked back at him. He had something down by his side, hidden in his hand. In his other hand was the *storage capsule*, or, as they now knew more accurately, the key to the gate comms system.

"I don't want to hurt you, Rob; you're a nice guy, but you guys don't understand. You should have let Mr. Terrell explain. I know the videos looked bad, but it's necessary."

Grant lifted his hand to show Rob he was holding a plasma pistol.

"The Centauri will come, Rob. We're just helping things along to make people see. You understand?"

Rob was considering if the wrench he was holding would let him take Grant out, but he had no decent place to kick off against anything hard enough to move with enough speed to get to Grant before Grant would get off multiple shots at him. Rob was in any case not a fighter.

"The entire system needs to stand together, Rob, and only Sovereign Earth has the will to power needed to do that. You get that, don't you?"

Grant moved closer to him, a pained look on his face.

"All I need is this unit, the evidence we broke into Vanguard, and to destroy the copies of the security footage. Nobody will believe anything without any physical evidence. But I hope you'll be with me, Rob. We've always gotten along, haven't we?"

Grant lifted the plasma pistol higher. He'd backed Rob up against the wall, seemingly without realizing what he was doing, as it gave Rob the leverage he needed.

Rob kicked hard against the wall and slammed into Grant. They were thrown into the opposite wall, and Rob grabbed at his arm and his plasma pistol.

Too late, Rob tried grabbing at Grant's other arm, just as he felt something hard hit his temple, and everything went black.

***

Mons heard noise coming from the storage bay on his way to engineering to help Clarice and turned down the hallway. It sounded like a fight, and he kicked off the wall to get there faster.

He was about to call out for whoever was fighting to quit it just as he got to the doorway and looked in.

Grant was standing over Rob with a wrench in one hand and a plasma pistol in the other.

Mons caught himself on the outside wall and clawed at it until he found a grip and pulled himself to the side. But it was too late.

"Is that you, Mons? Let me explain. I know you have sympathy for Sovereign Earth too."

188

It was true he had sympathies for the Sovereign Earth cause. Still had sympathy for the goal of uniting the system to be stronger. But what made him support that goal had made him fundamentally disgusted when he realized what Terrell was up to.

"Look, I know Terrell lied. But he had to. This cause is too important."

Mons hadn't quite given up on Sovereign Earth, but he'd given up on Terrell. Authority mattered to Mons. But so did integrity, and it was clear to him Terrell didn't have any. But he was not about to argue with Grant.

"That doesn't explain why Rob is unconscious, Grant," Mons said cautiously, while he considered his options.

"I know. I know. He caught me trying to take the capsule . . . Listen, whatever you think of Terrell, our only shot is to hand over every scrap of evidence that could potentially reveal them and convince him we've deleted the security footage. It's the right thing to do. If we don't, we'll all be killed anyway."

"I admit I've thought the same."

Mons was always a pragmatist. Of course he had considered that option. Their lives came first. The life of the captain in particular. His promise to submit to Zo's leadership mattered deeply to Mons. He outright treasured it and derived a great deal of satisfaction from it.

"You must feel the same. I know you saw me check the comms log for any messages about Vanguard, and you didn't say anything."

Mons had not realized at all that was what Grant was doing, but he didn't feel compelled to share.

"How about the sabotage, Grant? Was that you too? Smart move, if it was. You wanted to prevent the captain from rushing into broadcasting anything, *huh*?"

"I knew you'd get it! I snuck the spares out of storage and shorted a couple of lines on the board in the chaos while we were preparing to leave. The sneaking around worried me . . . I wanted to make sure there was time to talk Zo around."

"Did you know what Terrell was up to, Grant? Did he pay you?"

"Don't be stupid. I had no idea. I don't like it either. But it is what it is, and it was clearly necessary—you've seen how the captain reacted."

189

Mons pulled the knife he kept concealed in his boots quietly as he slid up to the doorway to face Grant.

"So, Grant, what is the plan? There's no way we can keep Rob's *accident* from the captain until after we've docked. We need a plan."

"I'm glad you see sense, Mons. It'll significantly improve our chances of convincing the captain this is necessary. I don't want to hurt her. I like Zo. I'm sure we can make her see sense together."

Grant's face was contorted in anger, but he didn't seem to be worried about Mons, and Mons slid inside, and looked Grant straight in the eyes.

"A little mutiny, then. You know she won't agree. And you know Vincent, Jonas, and Clarice won't budge. How are the two of us going to stop them?"

Mons slowly lifted his arm, as if to support himself on the wall, with the knife up his sleeve.

Grant turned toward Rob, and Mons instinctively instantly took his chance. He grabbed Grant by the throat and reached around and plunged the knife into Grant's abdomen. The blood sprayed everywhere and was floating all around the room and coalescing as they hit objects and bounced, surface tension managing to keep more and more of the fine mist together in bigger droplets.

Grant screamed, but the scream was muffled as Mons choked him as hard as he could. Grant was much stronger, but his strength was quickly dissipating as the blood loss started affecting him.

"You don't *get it*, do you, Grant?"

Grant dropped his plasma pistol and wrench and they were floating their next to him as he got weaker.

"I *did* think the same as you . . . At first."

"But Terrell will never let us go. As long as we're alive, we can talk, and the key becomes useless. And at the very least he'd face unwanted attention. You *never think ahead*."

As Grant stopped fighting, Mons grabbed the first aid kit and started trying to patch Grant up with sealing gel. He didn't want Grant to die. Not even now.

"Terrell cares about loyalty, Grant. You don't get that, do you?"

Mons' voice got shrill as a sense of desperation rose in his throat.

"It doesn't matter what we do now. He'll want us dead no matter what. He'd never trust any promise we make. No matter how thoroughly we clean the data off our systems."

That Grant didn't understand this made Mons' pity him for his naivety more than anything, as his hands were covered in Grant's blood.

Mons had never stabbed anyone with a knife. It was so much messier than a plasma pistol or rifle from a distance. Color drained from his face as he realized Grant was fading fast despite his efforts to stem the bleeding, and he felt like he was going to be sick.

He moved desperately and fast, not sure what he was doing. It seemed like he had stemmed the bleeding, but he didn't know if it was enough, and Rob was still out. Maybe he was dead—Mons realized he hadn't even checked.

"We're all going to die," he muttered to himself, as he was pulling himself over towards Rob when Vincent entered the room.

Chapter 45

"What the hell."

Vincent reflexively sprung for the plasma pistol floating next to Grant, kicking off the wall as hard as he could and spinning around to catch the pistol and get his legs in position to slow him down as he was about to hit the other wall.

Grant's blood felt like rain on his skin as he pushed through the droplets.

Mons had hardly had a chance to notice what was happening.

"Stop right there. Don't move a finger."

Vincent's voice was gruff and authoritative as he grabbed hold of a hand-rail and aimed the plasma pistol at Mons.

"It wasn't me," was the first thing to come out of Mons' mouth.

"Well, Grant was me, but he'd taken Rob out. He wants to plead our case to Terrell."

"You'd be a hell of a lot more convincing if Grant's blood wasn't all over us both. Back off."

Vincent slid over to Grant, the gun still aimed firmly at Mons' torso. He looked over his wound. The bleeding had been stemmed, but from what Vincent could tell, Mons had done a shit job. Maybe on purpose. Blood was pooling in the wound—Grant was still rapidly bleeding out; the blood was just contained in the wound and quite likely in his abdominal cavity.

There was nothing Vincent could do as long as Rob was out or worse, and he had to keep Mons in check. He floated over to the comm panel on the wall.

"Whoever is near the storage bay, Rob and Grant are down; I found Mons here with them."

"You traitor—you'll be lucky if we throw you out the damn airlock after this!"

Vincent slid over to Rob, and looked him over while Mons was quietly watching, showing no signs of remorse but also no sign of wanting to try anything. Rob's temple was bruised and swollen, but there was no other visible damage. He grabbed the first aid kit and pulled out one of the emergency stimulants and injected Rob, hoping he wasn't making things worse.

He glared at Mons.

"I promise, Vincent, it's not my fault. It's all Grant." Mons was practically whimpering.

How Mons managed to cower in zero-g, Vincent didn't quite understand, but Mons looked pitiful. It was hard to understand how he'd even gotten it together to hurt Grant like that. And Rob too.

Rob was stirring.

"Take it easy, Rob."

Vincent didn't really know anything else to say.

"There's no rush. I have him under control."

Vincent wanted to ask him to have a look at Grant, but he knew Rob was in no condition to move yet, and he was also certain it was too late for Grant anyway. Too late before he even got there.

Rob opened his eyes and looked around at the pools of blood.

"Where's Grant? You must stop him! Oh . . ."

"Are you saying it was Grant that hit you?"

Vincent relaxed a little bit.

"He was going for the capsule. I saw him . . . Then he launched into some rant about the Sovereign Earth cause."

"So you were telling the truth."

Vincent looked at Mons and lowered the gun.

"Sorry."

"I didn't want to hurt him like that. Will he be okay?"

Mons still looked sick.

"No. He was probably dead before I got here. You stopped the blood from getting out, but you didn't seal the actual bleed."

Mons vomited on hearing Vincent describe it.

"Oh, for fuck's sake."

***

Clarice entered the room closely followed by Jonas.

193

"Turns out it was Grant. Mons stopped him, if you can believe that."

Vincent sounded almost like a proud dad announcing his son had passed some sort of barbaric demonstration of masculinity.

Clarice couldn't believe the mess in front of her. Blood everywhere . . . A pool of vomit floating in front of Mons. A swelling bubble of blood by Grant's abdomen. A bloody knife floating around next to a wrench, and Rob still contorted and barely conscious next to Vincent.

"That surprisingly makes sense."

"What's that?" Vincent's proud grin made way for a somber look.

"I suspected someone had been sabotaging things. We thought it was you, Mons," Clarice said while looking over at the now slightly less cowering but still quite pathetic figure on the other end of the room.

"We?"

"The captain and I. We didn't want to let on we suspected anything before we got to the station . . . Didn't want to rush whoever it was into acting . . . Shit. This is our fault."

"You can't know that."

Mons had finally regained some confidence.

"Grant was ranting about Sovereign Earth. I only managed to get him because he thought he could convince me and he dropped his guard. If you'd revealed you suspected something, and started questioning me, he might have decided to take you out instead."

Clarice considered his words. He might be right. She wanted him to be right so she didn't have to feel guilty.

Rob was clear enough now that he moved over to Grant, and confirmed to them all that Vincent had probably been right—Grant had lost too much blood soon after the knife wound for them to have been able to stem it in time anyway.

Jonas grabbed one of the fluid evacuators and started suctioning up the mess.

"Feel free to help."

He looked around at Mons, Vincent, and Clarice.

Zo arrived as well, and Clarice explained the situation to her while trying not to be distracted with thoughts about the night before.

194

"Does that fit your evidence?"

"It does. It makes sense. I should have considered him before too. It just didn't seem like him."

"I didn't see it either, Clarice."

Zo put her hand on Clarice's shoulder briefly, before yanking it away. "Sorry."

She didn't need to say more. Clarice knew Zara wanted to give her space to process.

Rob and Vincent attached a bag over Grant's wound to prevent the blood from going everywhere, and started maneuvering his body to the medical bay. They'd need to pump the blood out of his abdominal cavity and seal it properly before bagging him up and sealing him in one of the freezers before the deceleration burn, or they'd have another big mess to clean up.

Zo pulled herself over to Mons, and Clarice watched her grab his shoulder and talk to him. She couldn't hear what Zo said, but Clarice knew what she wanted to say. She didn't particularly like Mons. There was nothing wrong per se. In some ways they were too alike. Neither of them enjoyed small talk or liked social gatherings much. But he'd always seemed sly to her. Always saying what he expected you to want him to say. Perhaps that's why she'd suspected him and not Grant.

The thought made her start feeling angry. Being misled by stupid emotions made her feel inadequate and worried she might have made other mistakes.

Chapter 46

Having confirmed there were no traces of the ship from Nautilus, even as they amped up their scans step by step, they were finally decelerating and making final adjustments toward Styx.

Naming the station after a river separating Earth from the underworld was a good indication of what people operating in the belt thought of being stuck out here. The station was a minor trading outpost locked in nearly the same orbit as a pair of the secondary belt gates, trailing about halfway between the two.

Belt stations led an odd existence. There were two major classes of them: the ones trailing or leading various gates, and the ones locked in orbit near major asteroids.

The latter were concentrated near the largest asteroids, or asteroid families, like Ceres, Vesta, and Pallas. The largest asteroids had stations present by virtue of size alone.

The Vesta family and Ceres were up to three stations each. Ceres had multiple gates in orbit serving as an interchange point for the belt to the inner system, and Vesta was on track to get a gate permanently following because the sheer number of asteroids in the Vesta family suitable to be transported in full was in the thousands.

Some slightly smaller asteroids, such as 16 Psyche, had stations nearby by virtue of the density of metallic ores.

The former class of stations served as waypoints, either in the same orbits as gates, set in between them, or in orbits further in or out, in orbits optimized for travel times to and from the gates, and on toward whichever ones of the asteroids or stations near them that happened to be near a given gate at the moment.

This made the fortunes of the gate trailing stations vary greatly depending on how many major asteroids they were near that month or year. Some stations were financed based on expectations of revenue from once-in-a-decade or longer situations where they'd be perfectly placed near multiple major asteroids at once, and would be near empty for months on end when nothing interesting was nearby.

With more gates being built and cutting the number of routes needed for sub-light transfers within the belt month by month even as traffic was skyrocketing, the latter were increasingly becoming hiding spots and locations for smugglers, pirates, and outlaws.

Zo had been to Styx before, and wasn't particularly happy to be back. It was a well-run station relative to many in the belt, with tight security and accordingly hefty fees, but she'd have preferred somewhere with less traffic.

But they didn't exactly have the luxury of being picky.

Zo was considering whether to dump Grant's body before they got there to avoid questions, but she decided against it. Styx C&C cared about what happened on the station, not what happened off it. They'd not cause any problem. They might charge a fee, that was all.

She had some experience of that, from when she earned the captain's chair.

Her biggest concern about Styx was more prosaic. They'd had to run out of Vanguard. They had to shoot their way out of Nautilus. On Styx neither was an option. The larger part of the station was the docking ring. Unlike on Vanguard and Nautilus, the docking area didn't spin. Instead, you were assigned a port and docked with it, and your crew then made its way in zero-g to an airlock in the central spine of the docking ring.

You then had to enter a transfer module that used a principle similar to a synchromesh transmission: the module would start moving toward the spinning part of the station while it would slowly spin up to match the speed of the spinning section, then dock with it.

It was a more practical design for a cargo-focused trading station. Some ships would dock and undock to receive supplies or unload cargo without their crew ever entering the spinning crew section.

But they would need to in order to find the components they needed or to buy access to the comms relay.

The downside was it provided a chokepoint. As long as C&C retained control of the transfer module, you couldn't get back to your ship if they didn't want you to.

Zo considered leaving some of the crew behind, but opted against it after discussing it with Vincent. If Styx C&C had an issue with them, having split up and being unable to work together seemed like it'd just make things worse.

They were just a few minutes away from docking, and they'd managed to get C&C to recognize the morse with their nav thrusters like near Mars, and had gotten approval to dock.

Clarice handled the final adjustments with ease, and Zo leaned back in her chair and just watched the monitors. She hoped this would all be over after this. Maybe they'd take some long, slow, boring freight missions in the belt afterward. Something uneventful enough they'd all long for more action by the time they were done, instead of dread every coming minute.

Maybe Clarice will figure out what she wants, she caught herself thinking. She allowed herself a little smile.

The docking was totally uneventful. There were only a handful of other ships docked along the docking ring, and they'd been assigned a port as far from the others as possible. Station staff being cautious, she hoped.

They pulled Grant in a body bag after them as they went to the airlock. Zo just wanted to get him handed over to be someone else's problem.

"Welcome to Styx. My apologies for the weapons, but you can't be too careful when someone claims their comms are broken. Most people have spare parts with them, you know."

"Yeah. Well. We did, but someone got rid of them."

Zo motioned to the body bag.

"Our documents are here. Including on him. Died in a fight following attempted mutiny."

The officer looked over the data Zo handed him.

"We will charge disposal to your account, Captain Ortega."

He didn't even bother looking at the body bag—just motioned for one of his men to take it.

"This all looks fine . . . You're free to go to the common area."

He pointed at a spoke leading towards the spine where they could transfer. He turned and motioned for his men to follow.

Zo and the whole crew kicked off toward the spine.

Chapter 47

The transfer to the crewed section of Styx took only a couple of minutes, as the rotation was relatively slow and so the transfer module didn't have to take much time to match rotation. Most of the time was, in fact, spent waiting for the airlocks on either end. They had the module to themselves, and when they got out on the other hand and took the elevator down to the concourse level, it was clear there weren't many people at the station at all.

The concourse level was a wheel not much smaller than the docking ring. The rotation provided a perceived gravity of about 30% of Earth normal. The size of the wheel was small enough you could readily see it bend upwards.

Compared to Vanguard, Styx was more claustrophobic in one sense. The wheel was narrow, and the roof on the concourse level was only about twenty meters up. But conversely, it felt more like being in a large mall where being closed in was normal, whereas the *ground* on Vanguard could sometimes feel like it was ominously closing in on you on the sides, like in a deep, steep valley.

They followed signs to the marketplace and identified someone who could provide them with spare parts for their comms system and half a number of other modules they needed.

Jonas found someone to ask if it was possible to buy data relay access, but stopped asking when he was told all data relay traffic had been tightly controlled since the Vanguard incident and encrypted traffic was attracting military attention.

The people he spoke to were all noticeably upset about the situation, and it was clear it was causing a lot of resentment. They agreed Styx C&C couldn't help it though—the news feeds were full of talk of heavy Mars and Earth military contingents entering the belt, and it wasn't safe for anyone to ignore it.

It didn't take long before he realized they'd attracted attention. Or not escaped it. At least two guards were keeping an eye on Clarice and Jonas.

"Clarice, discreetly see if you can pinpoint the security following us."

199

Clarice's eyes would give them an advantage, he thought. Unlike biological eyes, her apparent iris didn't tell you anything certain about where she was looking. Normally, it was locked to follow her simulated gaze, but her field of vision was defined by the full eyeball. Convenient when you didn't want people to know you were looking.

"There are four. The two obvious ones, but there are also two my infrared picked up hiding behind columns. Of course, it could be they're not security, but they act like it. Seven obvious cameras. Likely more."

Clarice whispered her update while seemingly still just casually looking at signal booster modules.

"You think they know who we are?"

Jonas looked for their best routes out. Of course, with the station layout the way it was, it was hard to imagine they had a chance of escaping if security wanted to stop them.

The documents they'd handed over used one of the fake idents for the ship, but their real names. As far as they could tell, they were wanted for questioning, but there was no arrest warrant out, and Styx was used to harboring far worse.

"They might. But given this place, the question is why they'd care."

Jonas spotted the rest of the crew coming toward them. He waited until they were close to discreetly point out the guards, while Clarice told them about the parts she'd obtained.

"So either the station is under pressure and being vigilant, or maybe it's Terrell."

Zo seemed relatively relaxed about the situation.

They were carrying no weapons—they had to pass through a weapons scan before the transfer module.

"We have to assume they're not in a hurry, or they'd have grabbed us already. My guess is they want to see what we're up to and feel confident they can prevent us from getting to the ship." Vincent was chewing on some protein bar and seemed like he didn't care.

Jonas knew he did, but he also was right—the guards had no reason to rush and try anything in this place. They were unarmed, the guards were armed, and they had no way of getting to the ship without locking themselves

200

into a small metal box under control of C&C. Vincent tended to respond with seeming disinterest like this when something really didn't matter. Then the moment it did, he'd suddenly be alert before anyone else even realized something was about to go down. Vincent's ability to switch focus like this always impressed Jonas.

"Let's grab a drink and let them think we've put our guard down."

Zo pointed to a bar at the other end of the marketplace, and they headed over there, trying to seem like they were just enjoying some R&R.

They were all on edge, and just sipping their drinks. The two guards they had spotted entered the bar and sat down where they could keep an eye on the crew.

After they'd ordered a couple of rounds and gotten progressively louder, mostly to put on a show, the whole crew got up to leave.

Jonas made a big show out of greeting the guards as they passed them. They stumbled and quickly took a right into an alcove.

"Are they following?"

"Shh . . . Patience."

Moments later, the guards came out after them, and as they passed the alcove, Jonas and Vincent grabbed them from behind while Mons and Zo gagged them and secured their weapons.

They used the guards' own lock ties to tie them up. They'd undoubtedly be found quickly, but at least it should buy them a few minutes. Or so they hoped.

Jonas led the way down the corridor to a lift. They were headed two thirds of the way up to the transfer module, where a secondary ring contained various plant systems as well as a backup bridge.

Hopefully, if they couldn't get to their ship, they might be able to get into the station systems from there and relay their data.

They got off the lift and started awkwardly jumping down toward the backup bridge in the much lower perceived gravity when two guards stepped out in front of them.

Chapter 48

"What are you doing here? This floor is staff only."

The first guard was a tall and well-built man and towered over the second guard. He held on firmly to his plasma rifle but had not yet aimed it at them.

Vincent stepped forward, palms up in a conciliatory manner.

"Sorry, we must have pressed the wrong button. We'll leave."

He made as if to turn around to leave.

"Hey, I think they're from that ship that just arrived. The ones we're meant to look out for."

Vincent had half turned, and used the opportunity to reach around to pull out the plasma pistol he had taken off the guards at the public level before ducking and rolling diagonally toward the rest of the crew, bringing him closer to cover and at the same time allowing him to twist around to fire. Before the guards even realized what he was doing, he was shooting at them.

Jonas pulled his weapon and was also shooting. The others ducked into an alcove.

"Charge, people. We need to rush them—the secondary bridge is that way and we can't defend this position."

Vincent was bouncing down the tunnel after the two guards who were retreating. They had clearly not expected to be followed so quickly as they had their backs to him and weren't paying attention.

He didn't like shooting people in the back, but in a fight, he was pragmatic first of all, and so he took out the smaller guard with a shot to the torso. Before the second guard had a chance to turn fully, Vincent hit his neck from close enough that his head collapsed down over the gaping hole.

The entrance to the secondary bridge was just past where Vincent had killed the guards. It was locked, but not well secured—they were easily able to shoot the lock apart.

Inside, Clarice went for the privileged access terminal while the rest looked for ways to secure the entrances.

Not having sufficient gravity to be able to block the doors with heavy objects was again a pain, but this time they had plasma weapons taken off the guards, and Vincent told the others to find suitable pieces of metal. First piece he took was one of the bridge chairs. They used a plasma rifle to cut it from the floor and again used the rifle to effectively weld the metal base of the chair to either side of the door. It wouldn't hold long, but it was a start.

They started dismantling everything they could find to weld to the door and across it.

"How is it going there, Clarice?"

"The system is heavily locked down. I have some access, but none to external comms. Found their email system, though. They've been in contact with Terrell. Looks like they're in with Sovereign Earth. Shortly after we arrived the assholes sold us out and asked for instructions."

"Shit. So if we get out of here alive, there'll be ships headed here."

"If we're going to go out, let's take these bastards with us."

Vincent had a very simple philosophy when it came to battle. Whether he thought he'd survive or not was irrelevant. His focus was to survive *right now*, and as a bonus aim to improve his position.

Right now that meant keeping Styx guards from getting to them long enough for Clarice to find a way to improve their position, and the talking was not helping that.

"We can do better with those damn doors, people."

Chapter 49

Clarice was frustrated. The noise as they were all trying to barricade the doors made it hard to focus; but more than that, she was frustrated that she was struggling to find a way into the system.

All her attempts to get into higher-security systems had failed. She was still stuck with access to their email, and even that was limited to reading what had been received—she couldn't even queue outbound messages.

She grudgingly mentally complimented their system administrator, but lacking access to other systems made her focus on their email, and she started trawling through them to look for clues to angles of attacks to other systems.

She found a number of links to internal sites, and hints to usernames, but was unable to get into any of them. All required two-factor authentication using tokens she didn't have.

She asked Jonas to scour the bridge for security tokens, but didn't expect to find any.

After butting her head against more locked down sites she was getting increasingly angry.

"*Hah*! I have something we can try. It's a long shot . . ."

Zo bounced over.

"They've not locked down station-keeping comms. We can talk to the other docked ships. If any of them are willing to relay a message, we might be able to get data out."

It was very much a long shot, Clarice admitted to herself. There were only a small number of ships on the station, and they depended on being able to contact someone at one of them, and then for that, someone had to be either willing to help or slow enough to sell them out to C&C that C&C didn't get a chance to send security to the remaining ships in time for them to try them.

Eight ships were registered as docked. One was theirs. Two were Styx's own shuttles. That left five to try.

She hailed the first one. No response. No indication whether or not they even got the signal out. She tried again, with the same result.

She tried the second one and got a reply from a very gruff voice. She explained they were having comms problems and asked if he'd be prepared to relay a file for them. They'd pay well.

"I don't think I should. External traffic is restricted at the moment . . . Which you know, or you'd go through official channels . . . Who exactly are you?"

Clarice cut the comms. She worried he'd hand them in instantly and hoped he didn't realize where the signal was coming from.

The third ship was a Mars trader. She decided to try to be honest. She introduced herself and told them they were wanted for questioning . . . Would he relay a message to Earth and Mars military?

"You know that attack on Vanguard that Mars was blamed for?"

"Yeah, I've seen the feeds. Everyone has."

"We have data proving it was a false flag operation. By terrorists that want to destroy the gate."

She could hear the intake of air.

"What do you want from me?"

"We need to get the data out, or we're dead."

"Sounds like if I get involved, I'll be dead too."

"You're already involved . . . Station command has told the terrorists we're here. Did you see any news about an Earth Destroyer named *Ariane*?"

"Yeah, destroyed near Mars. Some bullshit excuse about a training accident."

"It was the guys after us. Think you'll live if they come here before protection gets here?"

There was a long silence.

"Okay. I'll do it. I'll send your message."

Clarice plugged in her data storage unit and forwarded the files. The captain of the trader confirmed he'd received it and sent it on.

"Sorry, but I'm going to run. My ship is almost unarmed. Good luck . . . Hope you make it."

Clarice thanked him and cut the connection. Zo put her hand on Clarice's shoulders.

"Everyone. Unless he was lying, the message is out. Now all we can do is survive and hope someone acts."

As if to punctuate her statement, someone tried to force the door from the outside, and they could hear yelling in the corridor outside.

Chapter 50

It was clear the guards outside were unhappy that they were unable to enter the secondary bridge quickly. The voices outside got louder and it sounded like they were arguing over how to get in.

While they kept trying to break open the doors, Clarice reported she had to continuously fight against attempts to shut her out of the computer system.

Even though they had hopefully gotten a message out, Zo considered it essential to keep trying to break into the station systems in order to reduce the chance of a surprise.

Suddenly, the lights went off. They were only off for a brief moment before the secondary power supply kicked in. The bridge systems automatically dimmed to conserve power. This was the kind of thing that made Zo want to maintain a computer link—the secondary bridge, of course, had a backup system, but they had no idea how long it might be built to last for.

More importantly, they didn't know which weaknesses in the system the station staff might know about that they were not privy to.

For a station like this, the secondary bridge had almost certainly been built mainly to provide redundancy in case of the primary bridge being damaged, and they'd have been primarily concerned about accidents rather than factions inside the system fighting each other for control.

"Clarice, try to find out what they are doing."

"On it."

"I still have limited system access. No access to the power systems other than basic readouts. Looks like we should be good for somewhere between twelve and twenty-four hours."

"Great. By then we'll be either dead or have broken out of here anyway, so that's all we need."

Vincent grinned. Nobody else seemed to find his quip funny.

"I can try getting into the security cameras in the section and try to hack into them."

"Thanks, Clarice. Jonas, trace cables from the outside. See if you can figure out what, if anything, is hardwired into these bridge systems. With some luck, some systems have backups that don't go via the central computer core to provide extra redundancy."

"Of course, Captain."

Jonas went to work searching every part of the wall, both for visible cabling, and using sensors to try to track down built-in cables he could follow to a junction box or maintenance panel.

Outside the door it sounded like they'd agreed on a course of action, which wasn't good news. It was quiet for a while.

"Mons, check the ventilation system. Make sure nobody can crawl in anywhere. We'll also need to be on the lookout for any attempts to pump gas in."

Mons went to work securing the ventilation shafts, by welding the grates in place.

"Rob, there must be an emergency kit somewhere here . . . Look for any oxygen supply in case we need it."

Just as Rob was about to answer her, they could hear the next attempt at the door. It sounded like they'd somehow gotten hold of a small ship's plasma cannon to try to cut it open. The reinforcements they'd done wouldn't stand very long against that. They could see the metal heating up.

"Vincent and Jonas, with me, we'll need to be prepared to shoot through whenever that cannon opens a hole."

They took up positions on both sides of the door, waiting for the metal to fail. The plasma rifles they'd taken from the guards at the ready.

The moment the first plasma charge opened a hole, all three fired, immediately shifted positions, and fired again.

They could hear yelling and screaming from the corridor, unaware whether they'd hit anyone or just surprised them. The cannon stopped, and Jonas used the confusion to hold a metal drawer up to the melting metal where the hole had been punched, fusing it in place. It would hold only seconds once they started firing again, but it prevented them from trying to look in.

Rob came over with gas masks.

"I found masks . . . Even if they're not planning to use gas, we can."

He grinned much more than Zo had come to expect from him. It wasn't that he never smiled, but Rob always held back. He was a very cautious man.

"Whoever built this is highly paranoid. There's a supply of a highly active sedative here, enough to knock out the entire station . . . We won't get it very far without control of the ventilation system, but if we open the containers right after they punch a hole again, it should take them out."

Zo, Jacob, and Vincent put on their masks, and Rob went over to Clarice and Mons with theirs. Mons helped him move the gas canisters over to the door.

Just in time. The plasma cannon started up again. This time as soon as it punched through, they were the ones being fired at, but they were prepared and were well to the side.

"Now!"

Zo and Vincent opened the gas canisters next to the hole and hoped enough would leak out. The cannon kept firing, widening the hole, supported by occasional plasma rifle fire to keep them away.

The gas canisters were fully open at this point, and emptying rapidly. The shooting got more erratic. They could hear yelling and running in the corridor. At least some of the security staff had clearly gotten away when others started collapsing.

Zo moved closer to the hole that was now almost the size of a head, but she couldn't get particularly near as it was still glowing. Four guards were lying on the ground outside. She couldn't see anyone else yet, but others were bound to come, armed with gas masks themselves, and they'd better be prepared.

There was little they could do in the meantime. There wasn't much they could attach to the door that would hold up against a plasma cannon that size.

But one thing they could do.

"Vincent, you know the weak spots. See if you can destroy that thing."

Vincent looked out, and aimed at the plasma cannon, and systematically reduced the electronics on it to melted and charred lumps. It was very likely they'd be able to find something else to open the door with, but hopefully this would delay them further.

Chapter 51

C&C was busier than it had been in months. The station was almost empty as they were currently too far from any of the richer targets in the asteroid system to be of particular interest. The few ships visiting were explorers looking for who knows what, as surveys meant there was little new to discover, a few outlaws, and people just wanting to get away from something.

When the *Black Rain* arrived, they knew it was something special. They'd been asked to keep an eye out for something unusual and the urgent response when they'd reported it to Terrell made Pierre Fontaine, the owner of Styx, make a mental note to renegotiate their fees.

The ship hadn't identified itself as *Black Rain*, but the data they provided matched 100%. Pierre was annoyed they'd not realized sooner, so they could've stopped the crew in the transport module.

He'd yelled at several of his officers already and was looking over the latest reports. He had a team preparing to break the secondary bridge from the inside, and another was preparing one of their shuttles to try to attach explosives to the outer wall. If they couldn't cut their way in, they could eject the bastards into space.

It'd be expensive damage, but Terrell had asked him to do whatever necessary, and had been very clear he'd cover any costs.

"Sir, the fugitives used some kind of gas when we punched through. Four guards got out and closed off the section to cycle the air. Four are unconscious, possibly dead."

Pierre hadn't expected them to find the gas. He'd stored containers in both bridges as a last resort measure to pump into the ventilation system in case of a takeover or riot.

"So get masks on the teams and send them back in. NOW!"

He really didn't need this. He'd only signed on with Sovereign Earth for the money. It was inner system bullshit that meant nothing to him out here. Terrell better pay up.

"Ship on the sensors, sir. They're coming in too hot for a civilian ship. No answers to hails. They'll be here in half an hour. They must've been dark in the belt to have gotten this close without us noticing."

"Scan them and report as soon as you have more."

Pierre was getting nervous. Terrell hadn't informed them of any ships. If it was military and not one of Terrell's, there'd be no way he'd be able to stop them . . .

"Scans are inconclusive still, but it's big. Might be a destroyer."

"Hail them. Keep scanning and hailing until we have more data or an answer."

The ship had started decelerating hard at this point. His screens told him they'd have a sustained 6g minimum and still overshoot significantly.

On one hand that might give him some time to flee if needed. On the other hand, it might mean they were aiming to dump a full complement of missiles on them during their flyby.

"Styx, this is Mars Colonial Destroyer *Leonidas*. Mr. Fontaine, Aleph, Chronus, Rhea. Private channel."

Pierre's mood lightened. They may look like a Mars ship, but the message had given a code agreed with Terrell.

He arranged for the private channel and went to his office.

"This is Pierre Fontaine. Who am I speaking to?"

"I'm Captain Simmons. I take it you understood my message. For the sake of security, please give your response."

Pierre rattled off a number corresponding to the code words used, and the captain seemed satisfied.

"You know why we're here of course. I hear you have an *infestation* you need help with."

"Perfect timing, Captain . . . They've holed up in our secondary bridge. We're shooting our way in but they gassed my first team."

"Great. I just needed confirmation. I'm sorry, Captain, but I'm going to need this to look good. You see, they got data out, somehow. Now, to us that means either you're not loyal, or you're incompetent."

Pierre went white with fear.

"I promise, it was not us . . . I have no idea how . . ."

211

"Well, yes, that is part of the problem, now isn't it?"

"Mr. Fontaine, I'm giving you one last chance here. You'll surrender the station. We'll fire at you a couple of times to make it look good. We'll bring troops on board and announce your surrender. Play your part well enough that these rats come out willingly, and your station will take a bad beating, but you'll survive. Probably."

Pierre wasn't sure if he should trust the captain, but he had no choice. His display was flashing with warnings; the Mars ship had weapons lock, and could blow the station apart in a single pass.

"Okay, then . . . We'll surrender. I'll inform my crew not to shoot back. Please, try to limit the damage."

"We'll go easy on you."

Only seconds passed before the bridge was shaking. A rocket tore open a gaping hole in the secondary ring not far from the backup bridge.

***

A massive explosion shook the bridge, and at first Zo thought it was an attempt to break through to them. Everyone was thrown around, but once they'd caught themselves, there was no sign of an attempted breach anywhere.

"Damage control systems show a major hull breach further down this ring, but not particularly near us, Cap."

Clarice still had only limited access, but it helped.

The PA system sprung to life, and crackly speakers announced that the station was surrendering to the Mars Colonial Space Force, but Zo was skeptical. It could of course be just an attempt to trick them. The explosion had felt real, but who knew. And surrendering after one shot, even a bad one?

The attempts to break through the door hadn't restarted, however. She consulted with the crew on whether they should break out, but they decided against it. They'd wait. If it was true, Mars officers would soon enough check the secondary bridge and find them. If it wasn't true, well, they'd deal with that then.

Vincent looked out of the hole in the door and shook his head when he pulled it back in.

"No sign of anyone out there. But I'd suggest we still stay here."

***

They'd waited quietly for half an hour when they heard soldiers marching down the corridor. They even sounded more disciplined than the Styx rented mercenaries. Someone knocked on the door.

"Captain Ortega? This is the Mars Colonial Space Force. I'm Sergeant Jones. You're asked to please accompany me. We got your transmission. We're here to bring you in."

"Apologies, but we have some trust issues here, and besides, the door is jammed. Can you start by passing some credentials through, and if you seem to be who you are, we won't shoot at you once you have someone cut open the door. Sound reasonable?"

"Understood, Captain Ortega. We'll get right on that."

Chapter 52

"Sir, another ship is incoming."

"Ask Leonidas C&C to confirm if it is one of theirs."

"Leonidas says it is not. Advice is to treat as hostile."

Pierre was pacing and called down to the *Mars* boarding party from Leonidas he had surrendered to.

"I hope you can wrap this up . . . Hostile ship incoming. We don't know who. We're not in a position to fight."

"We know, Leonidas informed us. But your cooperation is noted."

***

"We're running short on time, Captain Ortega. I've been informed another ship is coming and we worry it will be Sovereign Earth. You need to come with us now."

They'd handed over documentation of their status, and according to Clarice it all looked like it checked out, but she'd spotted one little thing that worried her. The ship looked *too clean* she'd said. All the details matched up too perfectly. Clarice wasn't sure if it meant anything, but it could suggest a manufactured record.

But if another ship was coming . . .

***

"This is Earth Destroyer *Narcissus*. You are ordered to stand down, and under no circumstances interfere."

"Ignore them as long as possible. Interfere with what?"

"Sir, they've fired on *Leonidas*. A full complement of missiles. It's a Viking class, sir, it's twice the volume of *Leonidas* at least . . ."

"Monitors."

They got the battle with tactical overlay up on the main viewscreen. Fontaine had contact lens displays as everyone else, but he didn't like them.

214

He thought they didn't feel real. Really, he'd preferred windows, but for a battle in space that made no sense.

They had a prime view as *Narcissus* destroyed one of the main drives and several weapons platforms on *Leonidas*. *Leonidas* fired back, but they were struggling to adjust position, and the awkward launch position of their missiles gave *Narcissus* valuable extra seconds to track and destroy the missiles with its rail guns before the same guns were directed towards *Leonidas*.

They tore a wide gap in the side of the smaller destroyer, but had to take evasive action when *Leonidas* fired a second volley of missiles from a shorter distance and more direct this time. At least three rockets hit *Narcissus* and took out one of the rail guns and several plasma cannons.

Narcissus launched fighters. At the small distance between the ships, this was shaping up toward the total destruction of one of them.

Leonidas shot down several fighters but at least two got in too close and started strafing at *Leonidas* from point-blank range where *Leonidas'* own cannons could not hit them.

Meanwhile, *Narcissus* shifted, and the railgun started firing again, this time straight at the *Leonidas* bridge.

And then it all stopped.

"*Narcissus* has weapons lock on us, sir. And *Leonidas* informs us they've surrendered."

It was the last thing Pierre heard as he launched out of the bridge to try to get to his personal shuttle before the boarding party would get aboard, abandoning his crew.

He bounced down toward the elevator and used his priority access to override it. The elevator came back down, having been turned around, and was full of people trying to escape from the concourse level below. They started moving back up. He could feel the ride wasn't as smooth as normal. Shaking suggested *Narcissus* was either shooting or hitting them with breaching pods.

As they stumbled out of the elevator near the transfer pods, Pierre looked into the faces of a squad of Earth soldiers pointing plasma rifles at everyone.

"Sorry, but nobody is leaving until we've verified we have who we're here for."

***

"This is it."

The Mars soldiers were clearly antsy.

"Okay. We're coming out."

Zo figured if the wrong people were coming, being holed up here was particularly bad. If these guys were the wrong people . . . Well, they'd been in worse situations. At least they wouldn't be cornered anymore.

"Finally. Step back, and we'll cut this door open."

They had two people with plasma welders cutting from either side, and the door was open within minutes. They stepped carefully through the doorway to avoid being burned by the still-melting metal.

"Hurry. Come with us."

They were flanked on all sides by heavily armed Mars soldiers when the station shook again. One of the Mars soldiers got a message via radio, and whispered to the sergeant.

"They're here . . . We need to make it up to the docking ring and be prepared to shoot our way through."

Zo was annoyed they dragged things out. Maybe if they'd said yes right away they'd be gone by now, but at least they weren't fighting alone this time.

They got to the lift, but it didn't appear to be working. Several station staff were there as well and opened an emergency stairwell. It'd be a long climb, but in the very low gravity it would be fine—they'd be able to take large upwards leaps.

Soon, they were bouncing upward toward the central spine holding the transfer module.

They were getting close when they heard gunfire but couldn't see anything above.

The people above them in the shaft stopped. The Mars soldiers wanted to press ahead and were yelling at the people further up to move aside.

"Get out of the way or we'll move you out of the way."

They started pushing ahead. Someone didn't move fast enough and the sergeant hit him with his weapon and made him start falling slowly down the shaft.

"What are you doing?"

Zo looked at him in horror.

"It's us or them . . . *Deal with it.*"

The sergeant kept pushing up, and people were jumping out of his way as fast as they could.

The gunfire was getting louder.

Suddenly, the dead body of one of the station security staff fell past them in slow motion.

"Everyone keep weapons at the ready, we're almost there."

The admonition was unnecessary considering the shootout going on above. Given the falling soldier, the door from the maintenance shaft was clearly open, and there was a very real risk someone might think to shoot down the shaft at any moment.

The sergeant reached the top. He looked out carefully and motioned for them to follow.

Chapter 53

As soon as the sergeant stepped out, they heard more gunfire.

When Zo followed him out, she faced carnage. With zero gravity, there were bodies floating, pools of blood, and the sergeant's head flew past her.

She turned to yell a warning to the rest, but someone grabbed her and held a hand over her mouth.

"I wouldn't do that if you want to live."

Someone took her weapon off her, and she watched as more of her crew came up and were pulled aside.

"Stay calm. We're on your side."

Zo didn't know whether to trust them, but on the other hand, they had only shot at the people in the Mars uniforms, and while she tried struggling, she got nowhere.

"I don't know who these scum in Mars uniforms are, but they're not regulars. I don't think they're Mars soldiers at all." Zo's captor was whispering to her, and it made her relax a bit.

She watched two more of the "Mars" soldiers get shot in front of her before all of her crew were up, and they started pulling back to the transfer module. They were all bundled in. A small contingent of soldiers remained to guard them as their rotation slowed until they docked on the other side.

"Charges, please."

A soldier put explosives in the transfer module and sent it back.

"Don't want to be followed. Don't worry about my men, they've got escape gear in the breaching pod we came in."

For the first time, she was able to see his face. He smiled and pulled her with him toward one of the docking ports, and just as Zo was relaxing, his face turned into a gaping, burning hole.

Zo turned and saw a man she didn't know firing. Before anyone else could react, she grabbed at the weapon the soldier she'd been with had, and fired and fired at the man in front of her until one of the other soldiers with them stopped her.

"He's dead, ma'am. You got him."

They quickly checked the body, and all they found was his access card. Pierre Fontaine. The name meant nothing to her.

Zo's face was still covered in blood when they got to the shuttle. She looked at her crew. They all seemed okay. Clarice looked at her with a pained expression. Vincent looked down at his feet. Jonas, Rob, and Mons looked like they'd just surrendered to . . . whatever.

"Why are you here?"

Zo saw they had Earth uniforms, but after their last few days, uniform colors meant nothing to her anymore.

"The data you guys sent. We've been told to get you at all costs. Alive. You're wanted as witnesses."

Vincent laughed.

"I told you in twelve hours we'd either be dead or in a better position. They want us alive. It's a better position."

Even Zo smiled briefly.

The shuttle ride was brief. The Earth destroyer they were docking with was one of the largest she'd seen, and it gave her some sense of security. Surely not even Terrell had access to a destroyer this big.

Her smile grew wider.

Chapter 54

"Captain Ortega?"

As they stepped out of the airlock, she looked straight at an older captain in a clean uniform. A tall black man with a surprisingly slim build for a soldier, but she guessed being slim was more of an asset as a spaceship captain than muscles.

His height must be a pain, though, she thought to herself.

"I'm Captain Adebayo. I'm here to take you into custody. Your escorts have informed me you've promised to come voluntarily, so I figure we can . . . chat without so many people around first."

He motioned for her crew, and a couple of the soldiers with them followed.

"I'm all ears, Captain."

"First of all, I want you to know we received your data. I understand you've handed the original device to your escorts. Assuming it checks out—and given what happened here and with the *Ariane*—I have no reason to doubt you."

"So those people . . . They were not Mars Colony?"

"We don't think so. The Mars Colonial government insists they aren't, and the ship ident matches no known official Mars ship, so we're taking their word for it—they've been very eager to clear this up."

He shrugged. Zo got no sense of what Captain Adebayo felt about Mars, but she did get a sense he had little interest in escalation.

"Here's the thing. There's no way you can walk for what you did at Vanguard. You'll need to serve some time."

Zo expected as much. But it was better than being dead.

"However, opinion back home is that despite your unfortunate early assistance to Mr. Terrell . . . Well, you could've taken whatever offers he gave you and save yourself being hunted throughout the system."

He paused for a moment and looked straight at her.

"The fact you chose to use stun guns instead of plasma weapons during the Vanguard attack, unlike the other attackers, also very significantly went in your favor both as evidence you were not part of planning the bigger attack, and to show you wanted to avoid harm."

"So we need you to serve some time. But there's no appetite to make you serve *long*. You'll get a military advocate. You'll be offered a deal. It is my understanding that one of your crewmates was a Sovereign Earth supporter. I hear *he* was responsible for most of what went down."

Captain Adebayo raised his eyebrows and looked at Zo until it was clear to both of them that she understood exactly what he meant. Grant would be a scapegoat. Suited Zo just fine. Fierce loyalty to her crew, always, but Grant had betrayed her. And in any case, he was dead.

Zo felt a bit better.

"Regarding Mr. Terrell, there's a systemwide arrest warrant out for him for terrorism. It's only a question of time before we catch him."

"What about Sovereign Earth?"

"There's a probe." The captain shrugged and sighed.

"A probe?"

"They're going through all their finances and comms, and they're trying to freeze all of Terrell's assets, but most of it has been transferred into trusts and it may take years to untangle the legal mess."

"They also have lots of powerful supporters."

"But I wouldn't worry. They have bigger problems than you guys right now in trying to explain away the video and Terrell. You'll be protected."

At least as long as we're useful, Zo thought to herself.

Everyone else was quiet. It didn't feel like a win. But they had stopped a terrorist attack.

Zo knew what they felt. What if Terrell was right? What if they'd saved the gate, only for the Centauri to invade? What if this was really going to be the end, and they'd made it happen?

"Lieutenant. Put these people in secure quarters. Under guard. They're officially prisoners, but other than keeping them locked up, treat them as guests. Get them clean clothes and food and anything else they might need. Understood?"

The lieutenant nodded.

Captain Adebayo turned back to Zo and took her hand.

"Be honest, did you believe you'd all get out of this alive?"

Zo turned to look at her crew and family.

"No, sir. Thank you for the save."

Epilogue

"Good morning, Captain Ortega."

The man at the other end of the table was a Mr. Richards. Her lawyer. A short, stocky man. Balding. In a well-fitted suit.

Next to him was a military officer. A colonel. She couldn't quite remember his name, but they'd met before, briefly during one of the many debriefings.

"This is Colonel Williams."

"We've met."

"I have good news. The colonel has an offer for you."

"We did promise you'd not serve long . . . We have a . . . tricky situation that we believe you and crew could be helpful with," Williams started.

"A trading ship was attacked in Centauri space. They managed to get messages out and then disappeared. In their last message they swore the ship looked Centauri, and even relayed some footage."

The gate had been open for two months now, and the invasion Sovereign Earth had warned about hadn't happened. So far.

"Why would the Centauri attack an Earth ship?"

"Our thoughts exactly. It makes no sense. Given we have . . . a mutual acquaintance that likes to fake ship appearances who is on the run, we thought you might be interested in a commission to investigate."

Zo had been able to follow the news in prison. Thanks to their cooperation, they'd been allowed to serve in a low-security prison with all kinds of amenities. Sometimes Zo thought her cell was cozier than the cabin of her ship. But she missed her crew.

"The Centauri grudgingly accept a few of our military ships, but they're noisy about it. And if it's Terrell . . . Well, we'd like to catch him this time, and so we want things to happen quietly."

Williams looked straight at her.

"Especially given Sovereign Earth is more powerful than ever, and for whatever bullshit they're feeding us about having disowned Terrell, the way all his assets were mysteriously transferred into trusts benefiting Sovereign

Earth right before his arrest warrant was made public, we don't believe it for a second."

His voice lowered.

"I worry they have sympathizers in my team too, which makes it even more important nobody knows—whether Terrell is involved or it *is* some Centauri faction a leak would be damaging."

"So we'd be on our own?"

"Nobody would know except your lawyer and me. If you get implicated in anything, there's very little we can do."

"And our sentences?"

"Commuted if you take the job. Fully expunged once it's completed. All of you. You deserve it—I'm not happy you've been stuck in here a year, but we had to put on a show."

"And my ship?"

"As you left it. Better, actually. I've had a maintenance crew go over every part of it. It's better than new. We had a few . . . enhancements mounted. Better weapons. Engine upgrade. Reinforcements for the bulkheads. We can't send you out there without a fighting chance."

"Do we have a deal?"

Zo put out her hand and shook on it.

There were two things on Zo's mind. First, joy at being able to see her crew again . . . Second . . . The second was that she needed to see Terrell again. Badly. She had something to tell the bastard. She wanted to remind him of the story of how she became captain.

She usually felt sick to her stomach at the thought of what she had done to those men. But in this case, it made her smile. The thought of cutting Terrell apart limb by limb and cauterizing the wounds so he'd stay alive had sustained her. She started whistling while she waited for her lawyer to get the paperwork sorted out.

If you enjoyed this book . . .

First of all, I would appreciate it very much if you would rate this book and leave it a review. Whatever you liked (or didn't like), as it will be very helpful to other readers as well as to me.

Of course, I hope you liked this book enough that you want to see where Zo and the crew go next. If you do, then there are several ways you can stay up to date with what is happening with Galaxy∞Bound:

There's my website, at galaxybound.com where I post information on upcoming books. The site is also a blog where you can find posts about my writing as well as the occasional free short story.

My website also lets you sign up for my mailing list. I promise I'll send you *at most* one message per week, and that often includes early looks at new short stories and other material before it gets posted anywhere else.

You'd also be most welcome to follow me on Twitter: https://twitter.com/BoundGalaxy—I post about my writing as well as retweet lots of interesting stuff about sci-fi and space. And I'd love being able to talk directly to you there.

Printed in Great Britain
by Amazon